Poisoned
HONOR

Poisoned HONOR

A Broken Valor Novel

LEXI POST

USA TODAY & NY TIMES BESTSELLING AUTHOR

SUMMARY

After a near-fatal accident while on duty, Coast Guardsman rescue swimmer, Tyler Adams is determined to get back to work. Unfortunately, it has left him with a problem he can't conquer, a problem he must hide from the sexy psychologist he's interested in. But as more "accidents" occur at the Air Station, he is forced to involve her.

Dr. Meghan Haskell is thrilled to have landed the government contract to help the Coast Guardsmen and women in Crystal Waters, Florida. She's also impressed that Tyler has had no need of her services even after his accident. Smitten, she jumps at the chance to spend more time with him…until he asks the unthinkable.

Beyond frustrated after another crew member is seriously hurt, Tyler pushes every boundary to expose the saboteur, inadvertently endangering Meghan. Now he must overcome his limitations or lose her forever.

ACKNOWLEDGMENTS

For Bob Fabich Sr., who introduced me to the Coast Guard and the wonderful friends we've made. And for my sister Paige Wood whose artistic eye and creative mind are always such a huge help.

Thank you to United States Coast Guard, Chief Warrant Officer, Brian Hennessy for his ideas and for providing me with the appropriate links to the information I needed. Thank you to Deborah Emery-Gigliotti, MS, LCMHC, for her expertise from the psychological side. I was glad I could give my character a love story almost as great as hers.

In addition to all this help, I want to thank KC Crocker, Pamela Todd, Susan Staebell and Carolyn Derrico for their final look over. I couldn't have completed this without everyone involved.

AUTHOR'S NOTE

Poisoned Honor was inspired by William Blake's poem, "A Poison Tree," first published in 1794. In the poem, the narrator tells a tale of no remorse about how he entrapped his enemy with a poisoned apple from his tree, purposefully luring him there so he could have revenge for what may or may not have been a valid reason. The point being that the narrator is no better than his enemy through his deceit and anger.

What if one among the honorable were to become poisoned in this way, having been wronged but then feeding his anger to exact revenge? Would his deceit win the day? Would his traps bear fruition? And if there is only anger, can love still find a way to survive in such a poisonous atmosphere, or will the innocent succumb as well.

A Poison Tree

By William Blake

I was angry with my friend:

I told my wrath, my wrath did end.
I was angry with my foe:
I told it not, my wrath did grow.
And I waterd it in fears
And it grew both day and night,
Till it bore an apple bright.
And my foe beheld it shine,
And he knew that it was mine,

And into my garden stole,
When the night had veiled the pole;
In the morning glad I see
My foe outstretchd beneath the tree.

1794

CHAPTER ONE

Tyler Adams heard the snap above him as the cable he held beneath the MH-65 Dolphin helicopter lost its tension and he plummeted toward the raging ocean.

Fuck. He was too high!

Fear shot through him, causing his heart to skip as adrenaline flooded his body. With the rush of energy, his brain clicked into action. *Survive. What do I need to do to survive?*

It hadn't been the first time his life had been threatened and his training kicked in. He looked down at the fast-approaching waves.

Bend at the waist. Shit, no time!

His body made contact, but it didn't feel like water, it felt like concrete as his knees gave way at impact. There was a blissful instance of nothing as he plunged beneath the surface and then pain exploded inside him.

"Arrggghhh!"

Tyler sat up in bed. Sweat coated his body.

"Fucking goddamn nightmare." He rubbed his legs, the remembered agony of contact too real for any sane person. He wiggled his toes first to reassure himself they worked then bent his knees and threw his legs over the side of the bed.

Letting his head drop, he ran his hand through his short hair. Would he have these dreams forever? It had been four months since the accident. Why wouldn't they stop?

You have unresolved emotions.

The voice of the shrink he secretly went to hammered against his brain. He had only a week before he returned to regular duty. No one knew how much he dreaded that. How the fuck was he supposed to continue as a rescue swimmer when he'd woken in the hospital with a sudden fear of heights?

He glanced at the clock. 05:00. Today was his day off and he had an appointment with the shrink at 09:00. Maybe he could distract him, keep him from asking if he had the nightmare again. At least he'd convinced the Chief that he was fine, otherwise the government-contracted psychologist would never let him return to work.

Dr. Meghan Haskell was the one everyone was required to see if they needed help. He'd met her three weeks back when he'd given Drew a ride because it was raining. The kid didn't like getting wet and never wore a helmet while riding his foreign motorcycle.

He had the chance to see Meghan three more times, and every time he left he was glad she wasn't his shrink. There was no way he could tell her his issue. He'd be far too distracted.

Dr. Haskell was his age and stunning in a smart way. He always had a thing for gorgeous women in glasses. And she definitely qualified, grade A all the way. She dressed in a suit with a modest skirt, which showed off her toned legs in the high heels she wore. Her blouse was always demurely buttoned, but the profile of her suitcoat made it clear she had perfect curves.

It wasn't her beautiful body though that had him thinking about her more than he should. It was her eyes. They were a unique mixture of blue and green and they caught everything, his body movements, his tension, even his mannerisms.

That combined with her unique scent had his body paying attention. It was something citrus and spicy, like the tea she had in her hand last time he saw her.

She was always polite, giving him a smile. Class-act was written all over her, and he had every intention of asking her out *after* he returned to duty. There was no way he'd get closer to her beforehand. The last thing he needed was for her to figure out he was afraid of heights and tell his chief.

Even as he thought about her, his body started to

respond, which was a lot better than how it felt a few minutes earlier. What he needed was a quick two-mile swim and three-mile run to help him shake off the vestiges of the nightmare. Standing, he stretched his arms upward, pulling at the knots in his back, more remnants from his accident.

He'd been lucky with a just a couple broken legs. Alix Buchanan had it a lot worse. He still couldn't believe Alix was paralyzed from the waist down after her accident last week. Flying helicopters was her life. Her expert maneuvering of the out-of-control copter had saved the lives of everyone on board.

There had been so many freak accidents at the Station in the last six months that some of the crew members said it was haunted. Even Kolbe, Alix's co-pilot, had started researching the ownership of the land to make sure it wasn't located on an old Native American burial ground.

Moving forward, Tyler limped toward his bathroom, his awkward gait pissing him off. As the hot water sluiced over his muscles, his body rearranged itself in to better working order.

He grabbed the soap. Too bad he couldn't trade his nightmares for hot dreams of Dr. Meghan Haskell. He couldn't quite read her. Sometimes he thought she might be interested and other times not so much.

Maybe that was another aspect that attracted him, her poise. She always seemed so together. As a rescue swimmer, he rarely had the chance to see that. Any women he saved were either panicked or in shock though for good reason.

No matter why or how much he was attracted to the doctor, he refused to do anything about it until he was back on regular duty and had kicked his stupid fear to the curb.

Rinsing off, he let the heat of the water sooth his still healing body. He wanted to get back to saving lives. It was what he did and in another week or so, ready or not, he would return to hanging from a hovering helicopter above the waves. *Way* above the waves.

⌒

Dr. Meghan Haskell hit "save" after jotting down a few notes on her last client and closed the file. She had five minutes before her eight o'clock appointment. She might as well have another shot of caffeine.

She stood and walked across the fake oriental carpet to her cabinet. Opening it, she poured boiling hot water from her electric tea kettle over a new teabag and watched it steep.

She'd never been a morning person, but the government contract for psychological services she'd won required her to be available starting at six in the morning. The powers-that-be wanted their military personnel in the right frame of mind for duty. Luckily, she didn't have a 6:00AM today, but the number of

Coast Guard men and women coming in had begun to concern her.

Picking up her mug, she walked back to her desk. She wasn't complaining about the increase in clients. In fact, the contract had given her a credibility in the community that she had lacked as the newest psychologist to open up shop in Crystal Waters.

She took a sip of ginger-lemon tea and closed her eyes. Hmm, she loved the scent and taste of it, soothing while stimulating. Opening her eyes, she clicked her calendar open on her laptop. Lifting the mug to her lips as she scanned who she should expect next, she paused, the spicy aroma teasing her nose. It was Drew Linden.

He'd been coming to her the longest of any of the Coast Guard personnel. That man loved to talk, which made her job easy for a change. Her other Coast Guard male clients made her feel like she was pulling teeth with no anesthetic. On the other hand, those same males had completed their sessions. This young man, and he was young, really had no specific issues from his accident, but it was clear he wanted a sympathetic ear. That she could do.

Besides, it was the man who gave Drew a ride on rainy days that made her tingle. She glanced out the window. It was gloomy and wet, but it didn't look like it was actually raining. Would Tyler come? He always came up to the reception area when he could as easily just drop Drew off at the door. She liked to think he enjoyed talking to her, but he was so polite, it could just be that he wanted to be sure Drew made his appointment on time, since Drew had a tendency to flirt with the receptionist.

Even as she took another sip of what was soothing tea a moment ago, her body heated with anticipation. Tyler was the first man she'd ever met who wasn't a lawyer or architect or other professional, and she was seriously attracted to him. Not just because of his stature, but with his smile, his looks, and his big heart. She'd learned a bit about the man since Drew started coming to see her a month ago.

Tyler looked far younger than his years. She figured he had to be about twenty-eight based on the clues Drew dropped. She wouldn't be surprised if Tyler was still carded for alcohol. His blond hair was cut short, shaved at the base and sides, but a little longer on top. She itched to run her fingers through it like he often did.

As for his broad shoulders, that was the only part of him she was sure about since Coast Guard crews at Air Station Crystal Waters were required to wear their flight suits on duty, and Tyler Adams filled his out well. The loose jumpsuit hid his body except for his shoulders.

If she ever ran into him in a grocery store or at the mall when he was out of uniform, she doubted she could get three words past her lips. For someone with a doctorate in psychology, she could barely focus when he was around.

He had a strong jaw line with just a hint of a cleft in his chin. When she wasn't looking into his gray eyes, she caught herself watching his very kissable lips. Unfortunately, they'd only had a few short conversations. She wanted to know the man.

Not everyone was cut out to be a rescue swimmer both physically and emotionally. Plus, the fact that he wasn't sent to her after what Drew described as a horrifying accident had her heart fluttering. He must have nerves of steel.

Male laugher outside the building had her setting her tea on her desk then moving closer to the window. Oh crap. She was just in time to see Tyler smile at Drew and give him a friendly punch in the arm. That smile alone was enough to fluster her, but Tyler wasn't in uniform. She watched the two men until they disappeared under the awning, her forehead pressed against the glass.

Stepping away, she took a couple deep calming breaths. She'd been taught to always play it cool, let the other person reveal what they would, but being around Tyler left her breathless. Now he'd be in the reception area any second and she'd have to contend with him in a pair of shorts and a t-shirt up close. Even from the window, with her glasses on, she could see the bulge of his calves two flights up.

"Pull yourself together, Meg. He's just a great looking, heroic man. He'll never ask you out if you slobber all over him." Hearing her own voice helped, and she took one more sip of tea to help slow her pulse then strode to her door.

She paused and straightened her suitcoat. Drew often flirted with the shared office secretary outside, which always gave her a few moments with Tyler. A question about what he would do on his day off seemed the best way to start the conversation. She always liked to be prepared.

Opening the door, she walked out into the reception area and waited.

CHAPTER TWO

Within seconds of Meghan's arrival, the door opened and the first thing she noticed was the residual smile on Tyler's face from his conversation with Drew. Her insides warmed at the sight. The next thing sent her entire body into overheating.

Tyler wore a blue t-shirt that revealed his large biceps and strong forearms which were dusted with light blond hair and pale freckles. The shirt did nothing to hide the mounds of his chest or his narrow waist. She didn't even want to contemplate what his butt looked like in the shorts.

She forced a smile, but couldn't move forward, so she leaned back against her door frame to keep her from making a complete fool of herself. "Good morning, Drew, good morning, Tyler."

Drew nodded, but immediately turned his attention to the secretary.

"Good morning, Dr. Haskell." Tyler walked past Drew to face her, resting his forearm on one of the winged back chairs set next to each other in the waiting area.

She stared at his hand on the back of the chair. It was large, with thick fingers. He wore no ring, which she knew from their very first meeting. *Get a grip, Meg. He's just a handsome man who happens to be your age, unlike many of the younger men at the Air Station.*

She focused on his eyes to avoid the temptation of his body. "No uniform today?" *Well, duh.*

He shook his head. "It's my day off. Heading to St. Pete's Beach."

She glanced toward the small side window to her right. "Hmm, I hope it's not to get a tan."

He chuckled, the sound making her almost dizzy as it flowed over her. "It's going to clear up. By time I get there, it should be hot and baking."

And he would take off his shirt and run into the water he loved so much. What she wouldn't pay to see that. "I hope you have a lot of sunscreen then." *Really? He's a grown man not an eight-year-old. You keep treating him like that, he'll never ask you to dinner.*

Tyler nodded, a half smile remaining on his lips. "Sure do. I'm all about safety." He winked.

Why did the image of a condom float into her mind? She needed to focus. "I haven't been to the beach in so long. You'd think now that I live so close to the ocean, I'd be able to make time."

"Don't you get weekends off?" He looked disappointed, which caused her stomach to ping with hope.

"I do, if I keep up with my notes during the week. You're right. I need to go to the beach, even if it's just one close by. They may not be St. Pete's, but I don't need a crowd, just sand, sun, and water."

He broke into a wide smile. "Exactly. Back home in Maine, we have more rocky beaches than sandy ones, but they're all great." He glanced at his waterproof watch. "Well, I better get going, it's a good two-hour drive and I want to make the most of the day. Already had my caffeine, breakfast, swim and my run. Don't want to slow down now."

"Of course. Oh, so you won't be here to bring Drew to the base?" *Another really intelligent question, Meg. Nice job.*

"No, I roped Leo into playing chauffer to get the kid there. Leo's on duty today so he'll be here in about an hour."

Leonard was another Coast Guardsmen she had seen as a patient. "I hope we don't keep him waiting. Last I checked, I had an appointment." She nodded her head toward Drew, who was oblivious to their conversation. Then she gave Tyler a smile. "Have fun today."

He grinned. "Plan to." He turned then and as he passed Drew, nudged the man with his shoulder.

"Hey, watch where you're going."

"And you watch your time." Tyler's voice was stern, which sent a new heat pulsing through her body, but she focused on Drew.

That kind of treatment was one of the reasons Drew came to her—to complain, but from what she just witnessed, he brought it on himself sometimes. "Drew?"

"Coming Doc."

She didn't wait for him to finish with the secretary. Instead, she turned on her heel and strode into her office so she could catch a look at Tyler from her window. She picked up her tea and waited.

After a couple minutes, he emerged, striding confidently to his vehicle. She sipped at her warm drink. If only she had the day off. She could have asked to tag along…if she had the guts.

Since her last boyfriend, she'd been a little reticent to make the first move. That relationship had never had balance with him doling out attention like a treat. Luckily, it hadn't taken her long to see his pattern and break it off. That was the last scientist she planned on ever dating.

Just as she took another sip, Tyler opened the door of his truck and looked up toward her window. She caught her breath. Could he see her? Was the sun reflecting off the window or was she clearly visible?

When he finally stopped looking and jumped into his vehicle, she sat down hard in her chair. She had to find out if he caught her mooning over him. That would be too embarrassing. She glanced at the clock.

Eight ten. She would go downstairs tomorrow at this time to check to see if he could have seen her.

Wait, eight ten? She put down her tea and strode toward her open door. Peering over her glasses, she gave Drew her school teacher stare. "Mr. Linden, you're officially late."

⌒

"No more issues with going up to the second-floor training room then?"

Tyler grimaced as he looked away from Dr. Preston, the real reason he had to leave Dr. Haskell's so quickly. "I manage."

"Good. That's progress."

He looked back at the doctor and frowned. "It's pathetic."

"Tyler, you had a traumatic event occur. Falling from a second story porch can leave lifelong scars. "You're walking and back to work. That's considered progress in my field."

"Some progress. I can't even walk up the stairs without my hands sweating and my breath getting stuck in my chest."

"I think it's time you went to the Crystal Waters Mall to ride the escalators. They are much higher than the average flight of stairs, which would put the training room into perspective for you."

"Ride an escalator? I'm not a kid." He frowned.

"I don't treat my patients as kids. I treat them as adults with problems they can overcome if they follow my advice. Healing your mind is no different than healing your body. When your legs were broken, they started you with 'baby steps,' right?"

He nodded.

"As I thought. So, you've already taken your baby steps with the station staircase. Now you need to go higher."

He rose from the chair, curling his hands into fists, but he refused to look at his gray-haired doctor.

"Easy for you to say. You don't know what it's like. The anticipation of the fall. Then feeling like nothing is beneath your feet any more. The pain." He paused to dislodge the scene from his mind. "This is stupid. I'm *not* afraid of heights."

"You had the dream again." The doctor's matter-of-fact tone, irritated him. The man wasn't listening.

Tyler walked away, running his hand through his hair. He didn't say a word.

"Was it the same?"

He kept his back to the man, but he released a scornful chuckle. "It's no dream. Dreams I can handle. It's a nightmare. An exact replay of what happened. I get to relive it every time, knowing what's going to happen and unable to stop it. Even in my sleep the fall doesn't make sense."

"Tyler, your dreams are causing a conditioned

response in you that's not instinctual, or your response is causing the dreams. Either way, you need to break the cycle."

Break the cycle? Really? And he was paying this man how much out of his own pocket? Is this how Meghan Haskell would handle his temporary problem? Because it *was* temporary. He refused to accept his fear as permanent.

The doctor's toneless voice interrupted his thoughts. "You said it doesn't make sense. What doesn't make sense?"

He half turned toward Dr. Preston. "I always play it safe, double checking everything. There was no reason for me to fall." He had to be careful not to get too detailed. If the doctor discovered it was a work accident, there would be problems for him at the station. But the fact was, there were safeties on the safeties in the equipment. There should be no way for that line to have let go.

"What are you saying?"

He shook his head. "I don't know. But I need to find out why I fell."

The doctor leaned forward in his leather chair. "Yes, you do. This could aid you in overcoming your fear. If you can find out why it happened and know that you can prevent it from occurring again, you may have a breakthrough. Was there anyone else there when it happened."

He nodded absently. "Yes, three other people." It was protocol for there to be an investigation, but the Chief hadn't called him in to go over it. Why was that? Did Chief think he couldn't handle it? Shit.

"Then I suggest you talk to them about it. I'm surprised you haven't yet."

A new purpose began to take shape. He checked the line, *every* time. It was habit. Could the entire gear assemblage have broken? He didn't see anything when they pulled him into the helo because he was unconscious. "It seems an unwritten agreement that we don't talk about it. That's going to change." He strode back to the chair across from the doctor. The first person he planned to talk to was the Chief.

"But this doesn't get you out of going to the mall."

He folded his arms. "We're back to that again?"

———

Tyler nodded to Dr. Preston's secretary and strode out of the renovated old single-story Cracker building that was so typical on the northwest coast of Florida. He slowed as he checked his watch. He would have liked to have gone back to Meghan Haskell's office to pick up Drew, so he could see her again, but his own appointment had made that impossible.

Already the skies were clearing. If he wanted, he could go home and get his Harley. Unlike the kid, he wouldn't mind a few sprinkles because he wore a helmet. Florida might not have a helmet law, but he always wore one. It was safety equipment, like the kind that shouldn't let go in a helo.

But that would be another half-hour out of his day and he wanted to ask the chief about the investigation before heading for St. Pete's Beach. His whole crew had the day off, so it wasn't as if he'd find his pilot, Samantha, at the station, but the Chief would be there.

Pulling out of the parking lot, he headed for the Air Station. He didn't really want to go there on his day off, but he needed to do something immediately now that he had a focus.

He hated reacting. This was acting, forward motion. For the first time in four months, he felt comfortable in his own skin again. Why hadn't he asked the chief for the report before now?

The answer was obvious. He didn't need a shrink to figure that out. It was because deep down he was concerned that he might have done something wrong. Everything was habit, but what if he'd been careless?

He pulled his truck out of the parking lot and headed for the station. He always played it safe, something his dad had ingrained in him as a young child. As a logger, his dad had a lot of people working for him doing dangerous work, yet none of them had been injured on the job if they followed all the safety precautions. Those who didn't follow them were usually fired.

As he arrived at the gate, he pulled out his ID. The MP looked at him as if he'd lost his mind coming in when he obviously didn't have to be there, but he didn't say anything and let him in. Once at the hanger, he parked and went inside the steel building.

Ten minutes later he was back out. What a freakin' dead end that was. The investigation was still in progress and from his chief's choice of words, he'd bet they hadn't even started it yet.

Shit, it had taken them five months to discover that Drew's accident had been caused by weak bolts in the ceiling joist of the hanger. Drew was back at work, but he still saw Dr. Haskell on a weekly basis.

Tyler tensed. Why was the kid still seeing the doc? Because he liked her? Tyler didn't like the feeling in his gut at that idea. He shook his head. No, the receptionist was more Drew's speed. Dark hair, dark eyes and a rack that had to be fake. Meghan was blonde, aqua-eyed and real all over. He'd bet a month's salary on that.

Jumping into the truck again, he started it up. Soon he would return to being a rescue swimmer. It was who he was. Even as a teenager he was saving people off the coast of Maine as a life guard. It was what he was meant to do.

There was no way he'd settle for some desk job. He'd freakin' quit the Coast Guard altogether before pushing paper around or sending others out to do what he was damn good at himself. He had to get over his stupid phobia.

As his shrink said, a phobia was an excessive fear of something that even he could see was unreasonable. *If you can find out why it happened and know that you can prevent it from occurring again, you may have a breakthrough.* His doctor's words rebounded in his head. *If* he could determine why it happened. It looked like the only way to discover that was to do his own investigation.

There were a limited number of reasons why the cable which could hold a horse would snap under his own weight. Those reasons fell into two categories, human error or mechanical. His crew was off today, so talking to them about that night was out.

Suddenly, his whole body came alive as if he'd had a few too many energy drinks. He knew exactly who could help him with the mechanical side and the man was only a thirty-minute ride away at Broken Oak Horse Farm.

Glancing at the road signs, he took a quick left then headed back the way he came. St. Pete's Beach could wait. Kicking his fear of heights was top priority. Besides, Ryan Crawford owed him a favor. It was time to collect on it.

CHAPTER THREE

"You sure you're okay with me giving Alix your number?" Meghan adjusted the air conditioning vent as she sat in the parking lot of Westward Memorial Hospital. The humidity had rolled in last night and it was already in the eighties.

Jessie's response was quick. "Sure. But just be aware, losing part of a leg is totally different from having two you can't feel or use. Not sure if I'll be much help."

"I think you're the closest thing I've got. Unless you happen to have a paralyzed female veteran staying at Broken Oak."

Jessie laughed. "Meg, we haven't even finished the bunkhouse. It will be a couple months before we open for business. Speaking of, any chance you want to do some moonlighting over here? I know Ryan is looking for a psychologist for one of the regular staff. He'd hire you fulltime in a heartbeat, with my recommendation of course."

Meghan smiled. "That is tempting, but I'm finally

doing okay now because of this government contract. Thanks for the offer though, and the favor."

"No problem. Alix can call anytime. It will give me a break from all the work around here."

"You're not over doing it, are you?"

"Oh, don't you go all big sister on me, now. I'm fine." A voice in the background made it clear Jessie wasn't alone. "Listen, I gotta go. Work calls. Talk to you later."

Meghan hung up and turned off the engine of her six-year-old sedan. She couldn't help worrying about her little sister, but Jess hated to be coddled. At least her sister was willing to help.

She strode toward the automatic doors of the facility and the coolness they offered. Her excitement over being able to offer Alix someone she could talk to who might have a more similar background had her picking up the pace.

In no time, she opened the door to room 212 only to find it filled to capacity. She glanced at the clock on the wall. She was right on time, not early like she tended to be.

"Come in Dr. Haskell. These gorillas were just leaving." Alix sat in her hospital bed as if she were a queen holding court and the four men in uniform around her were her devoted knights. Meghan recognized Drew, Leonard and Steve as they were or had been clients of hers. The last man wasn't dressed in a flight suit like the others. From earlier conversations with Alix, he had to be Kolbe.

She'd learned more from Alix about the Air Station than any of the men had ever told her. There were two helicopter crews of four team members. Each one consisted of two pilots, one flight mechanic and one rescue swimmer. Usually, the crews stayed the same, but not always. The day Alix's helicopter went down, Leonard, Emilio, and the mechanic, Steve, were on board. Her regular crew.

Meghan moved her gaze from the men to Alix and smiled. Alix put on a good front with her fellow Coast Guardsmen, but she was devastated by her accident and subsequent paralysis. She'd already confided her fears of never getting married or having a family, something she'd always thought she'd have. At only twenty-six, she definitely deserved it.

"Aw, come on Alix, we know you two are just going to talk about the latest movie hunk and trade recipes." The tall young man with dark hair who she believed was Kolbe, received a swat on the tattoo of an octopus that peeked out from his t-shirt sleeve. He grabbed his bicep. "Ow. Why are you always beating on me? Kiss it and make it better?"

"Kolbe, take a hike."

The man grasped his chest as if her words had hurt him, but the twinkle in his eye made it clear their repartee was a common occurrence.

Drew, his blond hair slicked back as usual, winked. "I think Alix is a lot stronger than the docs think she is. She just likes being waited on hand and foot."

Meghan tensed, worried about how Alix would take that.

"Yeah, dumbass, that was my plan. Get busted up for life just so I could be pampered. Leo, get him out of here." She shook her head but smiled.

Leonard, the oldest of them all, locked his arm around Drew's head. "Come on, you heard the lady. We were just leaving anyway." He looked at Alix. "Going up with Sam to do a manatee count."

Drew struggled and Leonard let him go, but followed with a friendly shove toward the door. Emilio gave Alix the thumbs up as he left as well.

Kolbe's gaze found Meghan and he wiggled his brows. "Hey doc, if she confesses her secret love for me, be sure to let me know."

She shook her head at the flirt before he laughed and made his exit. Then she turned her attention to Alix.

"Sorry about that. They aren't so good in civilized situations, but I wouldn't want anyone else to have my back." Alix smiled.

It was hard to believe the beautiful blonde with large brown eyes and a pert nose was one of the best helicopter pilots on the east coast, at least that was according to Leonard. "I thought they behaved pretty well."

Alix's eyebrow rose, but she didn't say anything.

Meghan pulled up the chair the men had pushed aside and took off her glasses so she could see Alix's facial expressions clearly. "How are you doing?"

Her patient immediately frowned. "Crappy. My father is all over this now and won't let it go."

"Let what go?"

"The accident. This." She waved her hand toward her legs. "He wants someone to blame."

She studied Alix. "What about you? Do you want to blame someone?"

"Of course I do. But until we know why my Dolphin went ballistic on me, there's no one to blame. And what if they discover that it was just a faulty bolt, like with Drew's accident? Or worse?"

"What would be worse?"

"What if I caused the accident somehow? Put my crew in grave danger? The helo was spinning faster than a twister ride at an amusement park. My crew had to jump into the water, hoping the whole ride didn't come down on top of them."

Meghan's heart constricted, and she reached for the woman's hand. "Alix, the fact your crew made it out alive is a testament to how good a pilot you are. Good pilots like you don't cause accidents."

Alix stared at her with hope, and Meghan squeezed her hand.

"Well, it's going to suck if it's some kind of

malfunction." Alix pulled her hand away and crossed her arms. "My dad won't rest until he sues the company that made the machine, or the part for that matter."

She sat back, crossing her legs. "That's fine. Your dad loves you. You are the primary focus for him and your brothers. He needs to direct his anger. And I'm sure by time the investigation is completed, your dad will have cooled off and maybe even refocused his energy on how to get you to the best you can be."

"That's a waste of time. This is the best it's going to get. The doctors keep saying they want to run more tests and that it may not be permanent, but they are just trying to keep a positive spin on this. The fact is, I'll never walk." Alix's eyes filled with tears.

Meghan resisted the urge to comfort her. This was part of the process that Alix needed to go through. "I don't think you should give up hope yet, but waiting for a miracle won't help you now. You need to figure out what you *can* do and plan accordingly."

Alix looked at her as if she was a monster. "Do? Look at me. I can't *do* anything."

Meghan stood and raised her hand then lowered it to strike Alix.

The woman immediately blocked her. "What the hell are you doing?"

She took her hand back and smiled. "I'm proving to you that there are things you can do."

Alix glared at her. "Big deal. You have no idea

what this is like." She gestured toward her still legs. "What makes you the expert all of a sudden?"

She sat back down. "You're right. I don't know what it's like to be paralyzed from the waist down or have both my legs broken, or have lost a leg all together. If I did have firsthand experience of all the traumas my clients went through, I'd be worthless to them. I wouldn't be able to learn from them and read studies done or firsthand notes about their experiences with any objectivity."

Alix gave her a guarded look.

"By not having had your experience, or Leo's or Drew's or even my sister's, I have the capability to bring you perspective and the best solutions discovered to date for dealing with your trauma."

"Your sister? Is she the one who lost her leg?"

Meghan relaxed, happy that Alix had taken the bait. "Yes, in Afghanistan."

With lowered eyebrows Alix half turned away, but kept her gaze steady. "How? IED?"

As much as she didn't like to think about it, Meghan had to. She just hoped Jessie didn't get pissed at her. "No, she was shot in the knee. The entire joint was shattered and the leg from there down couldn't be saved." She left out the part that it had been part of Jessie's torture. Alix had her own problems to deal with.

Alix looked away as she sucked in the left side of her cheek.

Meghan let her think about that for a minute then stood. "My sister said, if you wanted to talk, you're welcome to call her." She held out one of her business cards with Jessie's name and number written on the back.

Startled, Alix turned her head toward her. "Really?"

She nodded. "Yes. Here."

Taking the card, Alix stared at it as if it was an alien object.

"I'll see you again on Monday, but if you want to talk to Jess, call her anytime. She said it would be a great break from work." Meghan turned and strolled toward the door. She'd just grabbed the handle when Alix spoke.

"How long ago?"

She looked over her shoulder. "I'll let Jess fill you in." Then she opened the door and walked out. As she entered the elevator, she took a deep breath. Having so many physical injuries among the Coast Guard personnel was keeping her on her toes. It might be time to do a little more research on Air Station Crystal Waters to see exactly what conditions they worked in.

⌒

Tyler turned the truck down the dirt road with the sign Broken Oak straddling it. The road curved left past a stand of trees. As he passed it, he took his foot off the gas. The farm's namesake stood in front of the grove, a Live Oak complete with Spanish moss was split neatly down the center by a lightning strike years ago. Both sides of the tree continued to grow upward and out, making it twice as large as it might have been.

Now he understood why Ryan had told him he had to buy the place for veteran rehabilitation. To be split like that and still grow was impressive and a great symbol of what Ryan hoped to accomplish here.

Pushing the gas pedal once again, his determination grew. If a tree could overcome a lightning strike, he could certainly get over a fear he'd never had before. He slowed as he pulled into the parking area, or what he assumed was the place to park. The packed dirt in front of a large white ranch house with flaking paint had three vehicles parked in three different directions.

He stepped out and immediately heard swearing coming from the barn.

A female's voice followed the expletives. "Quit your complaining you overgrown ox and move it to the right two more inches."

"You're worse than a drill sergeant."

"Stop. Hold it right there." The sound of a hammer followed.

The male voice wasn't Ryan's so Tyler strode to the front of the house. When he reached the three steps, he kept his gaze on the screen door. He could handle three steps. The inner door was open giving him a peek inside. "Hey Ryan! You home?"

No answer. Tyler opened the screen door and walked in. The inside looked in better shape than outside. To the right was a living room and to the left was a room with empty built-in book shelves, a mattress on the floor and a chair with a lamp on it. He thought Ryan had bought the place six months ago. Was he so busy working on it that he hadn't bought a bed for himself?

Tyler continued through the home, past the staircase to the second floor and into a kitchen and dining room both which looked out on the back fields. Tyler paused. The view was impressive, the muted hills of northern Florida dotted by a grove of trees here and there would be any horse's dream.

When his gaze rested on new construction to the right of the house, he found the back door and headed for it. The sound of a saw greeted him. When he walked the ramp into the structure, he found Ryan on his knees, putting down plywood. His friend's dark hair was still cut in military fashion and his shirt was covered in sawdust. A quick glance to the left where two saw horses and a circular saw sat, explained the mess. "So, you traded in your wrench for a saw?"

Startled, Ryan looked up before a wide grin split his lips. "I'll be a gator's lunch. Never expected to see a Coastie so far inland."

His friend rose and limped toward him. Tyler

smiled right back and gave Ryan a man hug. When they broke apart, he stepped back. "What's with the limp? Last time I saw you, you were safely working in an Afghan Compound garage."

"You know the Army. You never get to stay in one place for too long. Wherever they needed a mechanic, that's where I went." Ryan scanned him. "Looks like you made it through in one piece.

"Yeah. Glad that stint is over. You'd be amazed at how many people don't have a clue the Coast Guard is over there."

Ryan nodded. "Civilians. So, are you out? What are you going to do? Want a job here? I've got plenty of openings."

Tyler shook his head. "Nope. I love my job. In fact, I'm stationed out of Crystal Waters right now."

"What? How long? And only now you come and check out my spread?" Ryan shook his head in mock disappointment.

Tyler made a point to scan the single square area. "Well, it's not like there's much to see."

"Asshole, come on inside." Ryan bumped into Tyler as he brushed by. "I've got some cold beer, orange juice, and a few bottled waters. Lynzie just went to the store."

He followed his friend across the back lawn, or what there was of a lawn. It was more like weeds mowed close. "Lynzie? Don't tell me you got married."

As far as he'd known, Ryan didn't even have a girlfriend when they met.

Ryan opened the back door, but spoke over his shoulder. "Yup, and damned happy about it."

Meghan Haskell suddenly flitted across his mind. He had a gut feeling she'd like this place. "Sounds like you've adjusted to civilian life just fine."

His friend opened the fridge and pointed at the selection.

"I'll take a water."

Ryan handed him the bottle and grabbed an orange juice for himself. "Yeah, I got lucky. I found a purpose and my old flame all in the same three months. A lot of the veterans coming back aren't so lucky."

Tyler motioned toward the back pastures. "This place is impressive. I'm guessing you're not open yet."

"Not even close. I still need to hire staff, finish the bunk house, paint the outside of this house and my first three horses don't arrive until next month."

Tyler motioned toward the back with his water bottle. "Anyone who gets to rehab here will be lucky. Wish I could have done mine here instead of in three different facilities."

"Rehab?" Ryan scanned him again. "Did you get shot overseas too?"

Tyler tensed, knowing that by talking about it he'd see it all over again. "No, I made it through that okay, but four months ago, I was being hoisted back up to a Dolphin when the cable let go."

Ryan's eyes widened. "Let go?"

"Yeah." Tyler ran his hand through his hair. "The fall broke both my legs."

The whistle through Ryan's teeth, made Tyler feel a little better.

At least here he spoke to someone who knew what pain felt like. His shrink was clueless. Ryan's rehab farm suddenly didn't sound so farfetched. "Actually, that's why I'm here."

"I knew there had to be a reason." Ryan winked. "But you don't look like you need any more rehab.

"I don't." Not entirely true, but he wasn't about to share his acrophobia with Ryan. He hadn't told anyone about that except his shrink. "Remember when you said anytime I needed your expertise all I had to do was ask?"

Ryan swallowed his mouthful of orange juice before answering. "I do. What do you need me to fix?"

Tyler shook his head. "Not fix. I want to find out how it's possible that my hoist cable let go."

"Aren't they doing an investigation?"

"Yeah, but it's taking forever and I have to go back in the Dolphin in seven days. I need to know before I climb into the helo if it could happen again."

Ryan studied him. "There's something you're not telling me."

Yeah, there was plenty he wasn't telling him. He didn't know Ryan that well, but he had saved his ass back in Afghanistan. "You're right. There's been a lot of 'accidents' at the Air Station in the last six months. Three have been mechanical and a couple have been just someone in the wrong place at the wrong time, or so it would seem. My buddy Kolbe thinks it's voodoo or something."

Ryan straightened, his face serious for the first time since Tyler had arrived. "You think it's more."

He moved his hand through his hair again. "Yeah. I think it's sabotage made to look like an accident. I need your expertise to figure out how these issues could have occurred."

"Let me guess, the reports aren't in on half of them."

He nodded.

"You do realize that if you're right, that means you have a traitor on base."

Tyler's gut tightened, every nerve-ending on edge. "Yeah, I know."

"Damn." His friend shook his head. "That's serious shit. Think you can get me on base by Wednesday?"

With Ryan's Army record, that shouldn't be a problem. "You were honorably discharged, right?"

"Asshole." Ryan threw his empty bottle in the trash.

Tyler chuckled, releasing some of the tension in

his body. "I can get you on base. You'll just be a friend I'm showing around. In addition to my accident, one crew member was hit by a rotator blade that came loose and one of our pilots was paralyzed when her Dolphin went down."

"Got it. I'll pull up the specs before I head over so I know exactly what I'm looking at. Your choppers are closer to navy ones than Army."

"Hey, anything you know about them is more than I know. If we can manage some time around the equipment without Drew or Steve, the two mechanics, it will be a lot easier."

Ryan shook his head. "Even if we figure out what caused these problems, if it was someone setting them up, then you'll still have to prove it."

Yeah, he knew that, but he was hoping they really were just accidents. "Let's take this one step at a time."

"Okay." Ryan held his hand out toward the back door. "Since you're here, you want to take a look at the place?"

He took the final swallow from his water bottle and threw it in the trash. "Of course, it's my day off. Lead the way."

CHAPTER FOUR

Meghan strolled into the hanger at Air Station Crystal Waters. "Wow, that helicopter looks bigger up close." She walked forward, fascinated by how different it looked compared to when it was in the air.

Drew brushed by her and opened the front door. "I can fix these birds in my sleep. Go ahead. Sit in the pilot seat."

She looked inside but didn't clamber in. Her pencil skirt would have to be hiked to an indecent level to make that step. She faced Drew. "So, this is the helicopter Samantha flies?"

"Or Kolbe."

"Did I hear my name? Are you swearing about me again kid?" Kolbe's voice came from the other side of the helicopter.

As footsteps approached, Drew frowned at her. "I told you. They all think of me as a kid. Kolbe's only a year older than me."

As the man in question came into view, she had a

hard time believing he was only a year older. He and Drew were opposites. Kolbe was tall, broad and had a chiseled look about him, but wrinkles around his eyes and mouth proved he smiled a lot, and his black hair was wavy and messed.

Drew, on the other hand, was slender, like a cyclist, with slicked back blond hair, large blue eyes, and full lips. His skin, though, was what made him appear so young. It was pale and flawless. Something a woman might want. Someday he'd probably be happy he looked so young.

"Hi Doc. What are you doing here? If you're looking for a date, I'm available." Kolbe held his arms out as if he were her heart's desire, but his smirk made it clear he was only giving her his usual bull.

"I'll keep that in mind." She winked as he lost his smile in shock. "I wouldn't want to step on Alix's toes."

Kolbe shook his head. "We're just team mates, but it doesn't hurt to butter up the best pilot in the Guard."

"She's not the best." Drew turned toward her. "But she is damn good, if you will pardon my language."

She spoke to both men. "I understand if Alix hadn't been so good, lives would have been lost."

Kolbe sobered. "What she did was just, well, above and beyond. Steve, Leo and Emilio wouldn't be here right now, if she hadn't forced them off that bird."

She could tell that the two men were still deeply

affected by the mishap, so she didn't break the sudden silence.

Drew finally spoke. "I was just showing Dr. Haskell around."

Kolbe gave Drew a look that made it clear he didn't quite believe him. "Sure."

"I *am*. She wanted to see where we work, so she can better understand where some of us are coming from after our accidents. We haven't all been as lucky as you."

The resentment in Drew's voice caught her attention. She had noticed he gravitated toward the victim mode a lot, but he was the youngest there. It was easy to feel picked on, especially with the ribbing he took. At least that's what it sounded like based on what *he* told her.

Kolbe crossed himself. "But for the Grace of God and my good luck charm." He pulled out what looked like a sterling silver medallion with a jaguar head in relief on it. He kissed it before dropping it back beneath his flight suit.

"Pilots." Drew threw up his hands. "Superstitious to the core." He moved his gaze from her to Kolbe. "It's a good mechanic that will keep you up there, not your necklace."

Kolbe gave Drew a genuine smile. "It doesn't hurt to have both."

She touched Drew on his arm to get his attention.

"So, you were the mechanic on the flight when your friend Tyler had his accident?"

"Yeah. That was just weird. One minute he's coming up and the next he's gone. We were so close to the shallows, I didn't think we'd find him alive. If you look in here, you can see where we operate from." Drew slid the back door aside.

"I'll show her, kid. The Chief is looking for you."

"Now you tell me?" Drew turned toward her. "I swear I'm going to be thrown in the brig one of these days because of these clowns." Leaving the door to the helicopter open, he stalked away.

She looked askance at Kolbe. "Did you do that on purpose?"

"No, the Chief really is looking for him, and I did just temporarily forget." The flirtatious gleam came back into his dark eyes. "It must have been your beauty that wiped the Chief from my mind."

She rolled her eyes. Kolbe was so over the top, she couldn't imagine anyone taking him seriously, yet he was a pilot. "You were onboard the night Tyler fell. What happened?"

Kolbe's face lost his grin, but he didn't reveal anything. He just shook his head. "I don't have a clue. I'm guessing the Department of Defense will tell us in the report." He lowered his voice. "I think there's a curse. I've been looking into the background of this station. I haven't found anything yet, but there must be some upset spirits of some sort for so many things to go wrong."

She didn't believe in curses, so she nodded that she understood what he was saying, but turned to look inside the helicopter. She didn't know anything about them, but just seeing the space Drew and the others worked in, gave her a better appreciation for their job.

"I sit up here next to Samantha." Kolbe paused to wiggle his brow. "It's a sweet seat."

She glanced at the two seats in front, understanding better how the crew functioned. Alix had been in one of those in her helicopter. "Do you ever go in back to help?"

"Haven't yet. If I do, it means things are really bad. We have two pilots for a reason. If the helo doesn't stay aloft, no one lives. Sam often does the actual flying while I oversee the mission, but I fly a lot too. Don't want to get rusty." This time he didn't insinuate anything, and she caught a glimpse of the responsible man beneath the flirting.

She stepped back. "What if Tyler hadn't rescued the woman from the capsized boat before he fell. Who would have gone down to get her? Drew?"

"The same person who got Tyler that night. One of the boat rescue swimmers. Jorge or Ernie. That job is brutal physically and the Coast Guard only lets those who can handle it get in the water."

"So, you all just left Tyler floating in the water

unconscious and headed back here?" She tried to keep the panic from her voice, but knowing what happened to the man from Drew's session, made her more empathetic than she probably should be.

Kolbe looked at her as if she was an idiot. "No. We have protocols. We radioed in to the station and the closest boat was dispatched. Even if we had a rescue swimmer on board, our cable was useless, so we couldn't bring Tyler up. We hovered over him and the boat crew rescue swimmer pulled him out."

There were a lot more technicalities to the operations here than she was aware of. "What about Drew? How did he get hurt?"

"Dr. Haskell? What are you doing here?"

Even before she turned around, she knew who that voice belonged to, the deep tones with just a slight northern accent. Luckily, Tyler was in his flight suit, which helped her keep her heartbeat to under a hundred miles an hour. "Hi Tyler. I'm here to get a feel for your crews' workspace. Drew got permission but was called away, so Kolbe was explaining things." She trailed off at the angry look Tyler gave Kolbe. Now what was that for?

A man with military cut dark brown hair and cowboy boots gave her a big smile. "Hi, I'm Ryan Crawford, an old Army friend of Tyler's."

She shook hands with the man. His grip was firm, his green eyes friendly. "Nice to meet you." She turned her attention back to Tyler. "Drew and Kolbe explained what happened with your accident, but I wanted to know about Drew's, Steve's and Leonard's too."

Tyler stepped closer. "I'll be glad to show you. It's over here." He looked over his shoulder. "Ryan, you might as well see it too." Tyler returned his attention to her. "I'll tell you the *real* story. Kolbe over there will have you believing in voodoo before you leave here."

"Hey, don't knock it." Kolbe's shout from behind them was good-natured, so she relaxed as best she could. She didn't want to seem rude, but she'd prefer Tyler as an escort any day, even if he did fluster her.

He walked her toward the corner Kolbe had pointed to then stopped and took both her arms to position her so she faced the open hanger doors. His hands on her were strong and assured. In her office, he always seemed a bit guarded. Here he was in his element.

"This is where Drew was standing, only he was bent over, rummaging through his tool box." Tyler pointed directly above her. "That joist let go and smacked the kid on his shoulder and arm. Broke it in three places. He's got some metal plates holding it together."

She stared at the ceiling. If that had been her, she'd have a hard time trusting this building would stay together. Drew never mentioned that, but he did mention Tyler had been a witness. She looked back at him.

He stared at the ceiling. "After that, we checked every bolt, screw and weld. There wasn't another weak spot on the whole building." He lowered his gaze just inches from her own. "The kid was just in the wrong place at the wrong time."

She swallowed, trying to focus her thoughts on what he said instead of on his fascinating gray eyes. "What caused it?"

He shook his head slightly. "The report said it was a manufacturer defect with the bolts. They were faulty and with the vibrations around here, they were just finally jostled into breaking."

Wow, no wonder Drew felt like he was a target. Even the ceiling picked on him. "You were there, right?"

Tyler's eyes turned stormy and he stepped away, running his hand through his hair. "Yeah. I happened to look out of the helo in time to see it happen, but not in time to warn him."

She couldn't help herself. She placed her hand on his arm. "It's not your fault."

He refocused on her and shrugged. "I know, but if I had belted the water pump in faster, I would have looked out sooner and possibly shouted in time."

Tyler's friend came up to them. "Mind if I stand here?"

"Of course." She moved out of the way. That was odd.

Tyler walked her back toward the helicopter, his hand on the small of her back giving her tingles all over. She was such a sucker for a confident man, and Tyler exuded confidence in his own environment. No wonder he wasn't quite comfortable in her office building. This place was him.

"Is there anything else you wanted to see?" He'd stopped and dropped his hand from her body. She wanted to reach out and grab it back, but she refrained. "Yes. I noticed there's an orange helicopter and a white one. Which was Alix piloting when she had her accident?"

Tyler leaned up against the orange one and crossed his legs. "This one. It's called a Dolphin and is the type we usually use. The reason the Jayhawk over there is here is because the other Dolphin sank. They pulled it up, but they are still investigating her accident."

She swallowed hard. Her sessions with Alix had been focused on her feelings now, not during the accident. "How did Alix get out?"

"She didn't. She made sure her crew exited before the Dolphin hit the water. In effect, that also saved her life. Emilio dove below as soon as the helo hit and pulled her from it. She'd been knocked unconscious."

Meghan moved toward the still open door of the

cockpit and imagined being strapped in the machine as it hit the water. A shiver raced over her skin. She'd want to be unconscious when that happened as well, but it was probably the actual impact that caused Alix to blackout.

Tyler's hand on her shoulder surprised her. She started and slapped a hand to her chest as she caught her breath.

"Hey, I know it sounds scary. It was. But we train for disasters." He squeezed her shoulder, which helped slow her racing heart.

She looked at him behind her. "Do they know what caused the helicopter to go out of control?"

Releasing her, he folded his arms over his chest. "Not yet." He closed his mouth as if he had an opinion on the matter, but it was obvious he wasn't about to share it.

"Did you get the report from the Chief on *your* accident?"

Tyler glanced at his friend, who had been inspecting the blade on the tail of the aircraft, but who met Tyler's gaze as if in a silent signal before he responded. "No, it's hasn't been completed yet."

Tyler found himself hard pressed not to take Dr. Haskell into his confidence. Her concern for her patients had brought her here and her questions were to help her understand their experiences. His shrink had never even asked to see a picture of the porch he had supposedly fallen from.

"Does it always take so long?"

He shrugged. "It depends. If it's obvious why something happened, then it's quick. The harder it is to determine what went wrong, the longer it takes. The military likes to be thorough." He glanced at Ryan to see he had climbed up to look at the rotor blades.

"That makes sense." She moved to the open side door. "Drew said you were in back here."

He nodded. "Yes. This is where the cable actually comes from. Drew was inside here." He climbed in to show her. "Right now, it's pretty cramped in this one because we have a water pump in here for pumping water out of a boat or ship that still has a chance to limp into port, but if we know there are a lot of people in a small boat or that a ship is already sinking, we take this out to make more room for the rescued."

Tyler leaned out. "Drew watches below when I'm in the water and communicates to Sam and Kolbe. That night, the water pump was in here because it was a single person rescue." He moved deeper into the helo and touched the pump. "There was plenty of room for the casualty, Drew and myself.

When he looked back toward her, she had climbed in and was right behind him. Her citrusy-ginger scent hit him full on and he took a deep breath of it. She lifted her glasses to sit on top of her head and stared at the pump then turned her body around to look toward the side door opening. "There's not a lot of room in here."

Hell, there could be a football field in here and it wouldn't matter with her so close. He wanted to wrap his arms around her from behind and kiss her neck. Even move his hands up to cup—

She turned toward him again. "I mean, if something went wrong, why wouldn't Drew have seen it?"

His blood cooled. She had a point. If anyone was in a position to do damage to the cable, it would have been Drew. Unless it was done before they lifted off. Or unless it was a defect.

He'd make sure Ryan looked closely at the winch. "Don't forget there was a basket laying right where you are and it was night, so despite the interior lights, it can be hard to see something like a frayed cable line unless you are specifically looking for it. There's also the glare from the search light which we had on that night."

She shook her head, her thick hair so close he could almost touch it.

Shit, he needed to get her out of here. "Let me show you." He crawled around her, brushing against her long legs as he moved to the edge of the cabin. Jumping out, he held out his hand. "Kneel here by the edge."

She kicked off her high heels and took his hand to do as he requested. She was seriously hot in that position, especially in her suit and glasses. He imagined her exactly like that but kneeling at his feet and his groin tightened.

"Now what?"

Now take me into your mouth. He shook his head and refocused on what he wanted to show her. He grabbed the cable at the apex of the winch that hung away from the helo over the door. "This is where the cable was. If the frayed section was twenty feet below you, there would be no way you could see it."

She lowered her head as if looking down. "Ah, now I understand." She leaned to the side, pulling her legs out from under her to swing them over the edge of the door and grabbed her shoes. "Can you put those on the ground for me?"

"I'll do you one better." He held out her shoe and she placed her foot in it. Then he did the same for the other foot. He hadn't meant anything by it except to help her out, but the flash of thigh he saw as she lifted her foot, caused him to swallow hard.

"I feel like Cinderella."

He took her hand to help her out of the helo. "I think you are far smarter than she was."

Dr. Haskell's puzzled look had him kicking himself. Did he say that out loud? "I mean, she didn't even go to college or anything." Great. Now he was babbling.

"No, I guess she didn't."

"And I'm no Prince Charming. I'm just a guy from Maine." Someone save him. *Please.*

"Hey Tyler. Don't forget you said we would hit the PX before you go on duty."

Thank you, Ryan. "That's right." He glanced at his watch. "We better do that soon. Dr. Haskell, was there anything else you wanted to see while you're here?"

"Just the break room. Isn't that where Steve got the concussion?"

Ryan stepped next to the doctor. "Sounds good to me. I can grab a candy bar. I'm starving."

He frowned at Ryan before opening his arm toward the back half of the hangar. "This way."

Dr. Haskell lowered her glasses back onto her nose and headed in the direction he pointed to, her ass in her tight skirt and heels tempting him beyond reason.

When Ryan nudged him and wiggled his eyebrows at her, Tyler quickly stepped to her side and placed his hand at the small of her back again. He'd met Lynzie and knew Ryan was married, but he couldn't help feeling territorial with Meghan.

Territorial? He stopped and opened the door for the doctor. If he figured out who or what had caused his accident, he might finally kick the stupid fear he'd developed. Then he could ask her out. Or better yet, take her—

Ryan brushed by them as they walked into the break room, jarring him back to the present.

"So where is this equipment that fell?" Her pretty aqua eyes peered curiously at him.

Somewhere in his training, be it his parents' or the Coast Guard's, he managed to answer the rest of Dr. Haskell's questions without making a fool of himself. By time he'd walked her to her car, he needed a cold shower before reporting for duty.

"Thank you. That was very helpful. I probably should have come here after Drew's accident, but I'm glad I now have a visual of where Alix was." She gave him an appreciative smile.

"My pleasure."

He watched as she pulled her long legs inside her sedan, then he closed her door.

She backed the car out and as she drove by, she waved.

He held his hand up in acknowledgement before turning to head back to the hangar. Instead, he found his way blocked by Ryan.

"You want her."

He pushed past him. "So."

Ryan fell into step next to him. "I understand she's still counselling Alix, Drew and Leo."

"Not Leo. He's done. He was just having some anger issues with his limitations. Now he's completely healed, so he's good. Why?"

Ryan didn't answer right away and Tyler looked at him. "What?"

"If your theory is correct and there is a traitor, possibly even someone who has been hurt and everyone who was hurt had to see Dr. Haskell, then she might have some insight into who our culprit could be based on her conversations with them. If you were to go out with her, you might be able to learn something that would help us figure out who it might be."

Tyler stopped just feet from the hanger door. "What? You want me to sleep with her to get information?" He wasn't sure if he hated the idea more because that would be using her or because he wanted to have a good reason to spend more time with her.

"You don't have to sleep with her, just date her. Have some casual conversation where you talk about your work and the crews. She might reveal more about them than she realizes. From the way you hovered over her, I'm guessing it wouldn't be a hardship."

He didn't respond. Instead, he strode to the door and went inside. Ryan was hanging the forbidden fruit before him and giving him a legitimate reason to date her now, before he was ready. It was far too tempting. He needed that cold shower more than ever.

CHAPTER FIVE

Tyler kept his cool despite the acid churning in his stomach. The pattern of accidents that Ryan laid out before him made him want to hit something. Instead, he threw down the photo and gave his friend an accusatory stare. "How did you get a picture of the cable from my helo?"

"I still do an occasional favor for some high brass. You know, work on their corvettes or Harleys. Speaking of, how's yours running?"

Tyler walked away from his dining room table where Ryan had a bunch of helicopter parts spread out. It wasn't like he ever used the table anyway. "Don't change the subject. You called in a favor?"

Ryan looked up from a winch he was fiddling with and grinned. "Yeah."

The man continued to take the thing apart, so Tyler stalked into the kitchen and grabbed a soda. His need to know what had caused the accidents warred with his by-the-book morals. The sooner they figured this out, the better. He still hadn't told Ryan about his fear of heights and its impact on his looming deadline.

"Good." Ryan stopped what he'd been doing and sat. "Okay, so tell me what could have cut the cable that held you aloft that night."

Cut? He ran his hand through his hair. "That's not something you can cut with bolt cutters. You'd need something that will saw through steel."

"If the cable got stuck in the winch here," Ryan pointed to a section of the machinery sitting on the table, "there would have been a jerk upwards, a stop and then, maybe it would let go. Did you feel any jerk and stop before you fell?"

Tyler sat down opposite Ryan as a sickening feeling took hold of his stomach. "There was none of that. One minute I'm going up and the next nothing but air."

"Damn." Ryan nodded. "Well, it couldn't have been cut from the door frame, as that would put the helicopter at an unsafe angle, and the end would look frayed." He pointed to the photo laying on top of his table. "That's a clean cut." Ryan sat back. "I'm afraid someone brought something onto your helo with the express purpose of cutting you down."

"Fuck." The realities of the situation went against everything the military taught and everything he believed in. "That means Sam, Drew or Kolbe cut my hoist cable."

"Yours is the most obvious sabotage and the key. Whoever is doing this is getting cocky."

Tyler reeled at the thought that one of his crew had wanted to kill him. They were a team. They had each other's backs. Even outside the station, they'd partied together, gone to the beach, attended a wedding. How could one of them want him dead…and why?

For the first time since he'd woken up in the hospital with two broken legs, he was glad he wasn't back on regular duty yet. He wouldn't have a clue who he could trust. He'd be risking his life every time he went into the air, even if it was a training exercise.

Ryan pointed to a round metal assembly that looked like the back rotator of the Dolphin. "I think Alix's accident is the key to finding out who it is. My guess is we can rule out everyone who hasn't been hurt."

"That would leave Kolbe, Sam and Emilio. The only common denominators are Sam and Kolbe." A strange mix of relief and anger crashed inside him at his conclusion.

"That's fewer than I expected. Makes the job that much easier."

Unless someone was a masochist as well as a sadist. Now that he took away everything that was honorable and therefore a given, the possibilities multiplied. Tyler held up his hand. "Whoa, not so fast. Someone could have hurt themselves on purpose to avoid looking suspicious or…" he ran his hand through his hair, "or one or more of these events was simply an accident, which could have given the traitor the idea."

"You have a valid point." Ryan pulled out a piece of paper with his hand-written list of the accidents. His objective observations were what Tyler needed right now.

This investigation of theirs was too personal for him. He might miss something. "We need to figure out which of these was a definite accident or maybe more than one was. Drew's was the first, then Steve, Leo, Alix and me. This is going to take some time."

Ryan held up a pad of paper with his notes. "Two of these events took place in the hangar, two took place on the helos and one took place on the tarmac with a helo. Anyone could have arranged for the equipment in the break room to fall off the rack and hit Steve, but I don't think the bolts in the hangar roof joists could have been replaced without cameras seeing that. There are cameras in the hangar, right?"

Tyler grinned. "Of course. Yes, there are. I've never had to review the footage, but there is a first time for everything."

"Unless the DoD already took it." Ryan gave him an apologetic look.

"They've reviewed Drew's and they might have finished looking at Steve's so that would mean the footage is back in the hangar. Let's go."

Meghan took the bag with the sea breeze scented candle off the counter and thanked the cashier. After talking to Tyler earlier in the week and visiting the Air Station with the Gulf breezes filling the air, she had a new yearning for the beach. It might be Saturday, but she still had errands to run and notes to finish, but with any luck, she planned to visit the beach tomorrow. She'd even worn her pale pink and white sundress to keep her goal in mind.

Walking out of the store, she lifted her glasses to look at her list. Two more items and she could go home. Both were on the second level of the Crystal Waters Mall. She headed for the escalator.

It was a pretty busy place on Saturdays, since it was the only mall in twenty miles. It was also air-conditioned and with the heat outside, it was clear many people were enjoying that particular luxury as there were very few children. Mostly teen-agers and elders.

As she approached the escalator, a funny feeling like she was being watched caused her to hesitate. Scanning the crowd, she discovered why. Standing in a pair of army boots, jeans and sleeveless aqua t-shirt with Crystal Waters, Florida emblazoned across his wide chest was Tyler Adams.

He gave her a crooked smile when she met his

gaze. *Okay, don't hyperventilate just because his biceps are bigger than your head.* She returned his smile, but couldn't get her feet to move. It had been hard enough being next to him in the helicopter earlier this week. Then when he'd slipped her shoes on her feet, she thought she would fall over. Luckily, having his friend Ryan there had helped her find her balance.

Tyler strode around the escalator toward her. He didn't seem as confidant as he did at the Air Station, but his good-boy turns biker look had her heart racing.

"Dr. Haskell, I'm guessing you have the day off too."

She glanced at her dress, hoping he liked it. She was rarely so casual. "Yes, just running a few errands. How about you? It's the perfect day for the beach, but I don't think those jeans would be that comfortable out there today." *Sure, Meg, criticize what he's wearing. Hypocrite. The minute he turns his back, you know you're going to look at his ass.*

He shrugged, his massive shoulders catching and holding her attention. "I wear my jeans when I'm on my bike."

Her heart started doing a tap-dance. "Do you mean like a ten-speed?" He was, after all, into keeping fit. *And my, how fit.*

He chuckled. "No, my Harley."

Her mouth dried up at the knowledge he really did ride a motorcycle. It wasn't as if he was from the wrong side of the tracks or anything, but the fluttering in her stomach told her she was in big trouble anyway.

She swallowed, hoping to get her voice to work. "Oh, I didn't realize you rode. I was just heading upstairs to buy some loose-leaf tea. They have a little coffee bar right there. Would you like to join me?" So much for letting the guy make the first move. She was pathetic.

"I *could* use something to drink." He glanced at the escalator before moving his gaze up to the top floor, the edge of which had half-walls made of glass. He swallowed hard then looked back at her. "You like tea a lot, don't you?"

"It's my biggest vice."

He laughed, the sound vibrating right into her heart. "Dr. Haskell, I'm not sure tea qualifies as a vice."

She felt her cheeks heat. "Please, call me Meghan. I guess you're right about my 'vice'. There are some great health benefits to some teas. Some have anti-oxidants while others can help your mind stay sharp. Some can be comforting like chai or English breakfast." Her glasses made his facial features a little blurry standing this close, but he must be bored already. "Why don't we head up. I'm sure you don't need to know everything about tea."

He moved to the side, to let her precede him. Always the gentleman. "Since I don't know anything about tea, it's all new to me."

She stepped onto the escalator and turned around to face him.

Tyler's jaw was shut tight and he stared at her as if he couldn't take his eyes off her. The fluttering in her stomach increased. "I decided to take your advice and go to the beach. Not today of course, because I have a few more notes to take care of, but tomorrow. I hope it's going to be nice. I haven't had a chance to check the weather. Do you know what the weather will be like tomorrow?" *And maybe ask if you can join me?*

Tyler didn't say anything, just kept staring at her. Maybe she should take her glasses off so she could be sure. She moved her glasses to the top of her head, effectively pushing her hair away from her face at the same time.

The first thing she noticed was that Tyler's gray eyes seemed to have lightened and looked a bit glazed. The next thing she noticed was perspiration beading on his forehead and just a bit above his upper lip. "Tyler, are you okay?"

She laid her hand on his arm and his other hand grabbed hers and held tight. He shook his head but didn't say anything. Something was not right here. As soon as they stepped off the escalator, she led him to the nearest bench and had him sit down. She crouched down in front of him and with her free hand touched his cheek. "Tyler?"

He blinked and took a deep breath, releasing her hand from his death grip. "Sorry. Got a muscle cramp in my back. They can get pretty nasty. Must have overdone my work out this morning."

"Do you need something?" It was hard to imagine this man, who was so strong and fit, almost paralyzed by a cramp, but it made sense in a way.

He shook his head. "No, it's going away. I forget to take deep breaths." He paused and took a long one. "That can really help clear it up, but sometimes the pain is so intense it makes it hard to breath at all.

"I hope this never happens when you are rescuing someone."

"What? No, because those days I don't work out. If I end up battling high seas, I get plenty of exercise. Like you just saw, I don't want to freeze up on the job." He gave her a small smile.

That more than anything calmed her concern. She rose, but he grasped her hand.

"Sit for a minute?"

"Of course." She sat next to him. That he wanted her there while he was hurting, made her feel closer to him.

Tyler took a deep breath as he focused on not squeezing Meghan's hand too tightly. He'd come to the mall to fulfill his assignment, determined to scare the fear right out of him, but when Meghan showed up, he couldn't resist having her with him. What a wuss.

What the fuck was he going to do next week if his fear didn't leave when he discovered who had caused his accident and he had to go up in the helo? He glanced at Meghan's profile, her attention taken by three puppies playing in the window of the pet store.

She was smart. He got lucky this time by playing up the muscle cramp story. He assumed she wasn't as in tune with workout problems as she was with a person's psyche. He seriously had been ready to throw up. If she hadn't been there…

If you were to go out with her, you might be able to learn something that would help us figure out who it might be. Ryan's words echoed in his brain. Did she know what was happening at the Station? She'd counselled three of the crew members already. That could be a big help.

But that's not why he wanted to date her. He really liked her, but if she figured out he was afraid of heights, he'd be screwed. He'd have to go down the escalator without her. She was too smart to be fooled twice. He glanced at the yawning opening of the atrium and quickly turned his head, but not before his stomach started to roll over again. "I think I'm ready for some of that tea now."

She looked at him, startled, her wide aqua eyes breath-taking. This close, he could see she had long lashes, but wasn't wearing any make up. With her blonde hair loose, just brushing her bare shoulders, she looked more approachable.

"Tyler, you don't have to have tea. They serve other drinks too."

He grinned. "I thought you could recommend a type of tea that helps relax me so I don't get any more cramps today." If it worked, he might just drink it by the gallon so he could get down the escalator in one piece.

She cocked her head. "I think there are a few different ones. I know chamomile is good for before bed, but I'm sure Celia will be able point us in the right direction."

"Celia?"

Her cheeks turned a pretty shade of rose. "Like I said. It's a vice. I come here so often I know who works what day."

"I still don't think it's a vice." He stood, and she rose too. "Let's go see what Celia has for us." He still hadn't let go of her hand and since she didn't try to pull away, he held on. It had been a long time since he'd had a girlfriend. Moving every two to three years wasn't for every woman.

"Here it is." Meghan pointed to a small shop that boasted a sign that read Tea Room and Coffee Bar.

"Why isn't it Tea Bar and Coffee Room?"

She laughed, a low, full sound that made him want to make her laugh again. "I have no idea. Maybe we should ask Celia."

He gestured toward the shop with his free arm. "After you." Letting go of her hand, he rested his on her lower back. The pale pink sundress didn't hide any of her curves. In fact, it made her look so delicate, it revved his protective instincts up a notch.

As she smiled at the older woman behind the counter, he tried to refocus. He had less than three days to find the traitor before he went back in the air. It was time to get the lovely doctor to talk.

Tyler glanced at the clock on his computer for the fifteenth time in fifteen minutes. It wasn't that he wanted his shift to be over, it was that he didn't. After tonight, he only had two more days before going back to regular duty.

His crew knew something was up and he let them think it was because he was anxious to get back to his job, but he was more anxious about who might kill him. He'd reviewed hours of camera footage but he'd found nothing. The cameras were mounted in the right places, but it appeared that they might have moved, which considering the vibration the hangar took, wasn't surprising.

He was sure someone probably checked them periodically, but he couldn't ask without arousing suspicions. Whatever the reason, there were spaces in the hangar that weren't covered and those places were just enough room for someone to set something up.

Ryan was more sure than ever that someone was causing the accidents. Though he hadn't been able to look at Alix's Dolphin, he'd gone to see her and had a really good hypothesis on what happened.

His need to do something had Tyler standing and looking out the inside window of the room into the hangar. He stayed far enough away from the actual window for him to handle the view without sweating.

Sam, Drew, Kolbe and Emilio were on duty. Emilio, the other rescue swimmer, wasn't on Tyler's helo the night of his accident, but he was on Alix's. There was no way he'd sabotage his own ride, so Tyler didn't even consider him in his search for the traitor.

All four were busy in separate areas as they had just finished dinner and were settling into their assigned duties. If there was no call, it would be quiet with only the five of them. But rain had already started beating on the metal roof of the hangar portending the severe thunderstorm they expected.

It was typical for this area of Florida, as he'd learned after being assigned to Crystal Waters less than two months. A beautiful day followed by clouds rolling in with the sunset. Today had been a perfect beach day.

Had Meghan gone to the beach like she planned? The memory of her asking him to tag along had him straightening his shoulders. She was definitely interested. Unfortunately, nothing in their conversation gave him even a hint about what his fellow crew members had talked to her about.

A strike of lightning hit close by, flashing the inside of the hangar like a strobe light. Thunder followed. Quickly, he moved to the panel and checked the weather. It was going to be a nasty storm, but was moving fast.

Footsteps on the metal stairs to the second floor let him know he may soon have company. The training room was down the open walkway, but there was no reason to go in there.

Emilio appeared in the doorway, his broad frame taking up most of it. "Hey, is this storm a big one?"

He shook his head. "No, it's a smash and grab."

"I'll let them know. You don't have any ibuprofen in your locker, do you? I just ran out."

"I do. Go ahead, help yourself."

Another couple flashes followed closely by thunder stopped their conversation.

"Jesus, is this thing going out or heading in?" Emilio pointed to the panel.

"It's moving in." Tyler looked at the panel more closely. "We've already got twelve-foot seas in the Gulf, but the weather should calm down once this moves farther inland. I'm not seeing anything but some light showers after this cell goes by."

"Good. I don't mind if—"

"MAYDAY! MAYDAY! This is the Daydreamer I've lost both my engines and the bilge pump isn't working. We're getting beaten up out here. I think we're going down."

Tyler grabbed the radio. "This is Sector Crystal Waters. What is your location? Out."

There was no response and he looked at Emilio. "Get everyone ready to go. I'll contact the surface crew and see if I can't get more info."

"Right."

After letting the boat crew know there would be a SAR, Search and Rescue, he got back on the radio. "Daydreamer, what is your location? Repeat. We need your location. Out."

Again, silence greeted him. Where the hell were they?

"Daydreamer, what was your last known location? Out."

"We are definitely going down. I've got three passengers. Fuck, this is a forty-foot boat."

"Daydreamer, tell me your last known location. Out."

"Right. Uh, I'm not sure. We left Seminole Island after dinner. Wanted to beat the storm. We were trying to get to Crescent Cove. I had her going full steam until we came down hard and we flooded."

"Listen to me. We're going to find you. Do you have EPIRBs and life jackets? Out."

"We have life jackets, but no EPIRBs."

Shit. With no Emergency Position Indicating Radio Beacons, it was going to be tough to find these people. "Okay, if the boat is definitely sinking, you need to jump off before it's completely submerged. Out."

"Fuck. We gotta go now. You gotta find us."

"We will. We have a helicopter in the air and a cutter on the way. Out."

There was no response. He stood at the sound of the hangar doors opening. Wind and rain whipped into the hangar as the Dolphin MH-65 was pulled out by the mule. In no time, Sam had the rotator blades going.

Emilio and Drew closed the doors and Tyler heard the helo take off in the storm. Now all he could do was wait. Everything the Daydreamer had said was patched through to Sam, so she'd know where to head.

He moved back to his computer and did some calculations and relayed the estimated coordinates, give or take a few miles depending on how bad the storm had thrown the boat off course.

If any other calls came in now, he'd have to call their sister station. He listened to the radio communications between Kolbe and the cutter called the Apalachee. He wanted to be out there. After more than four months away, he yearned for the challenge. To be in the helo with—Shit.

Suddenly, his concern moved from the people in the water to the crew of the Dolphin. Would they all make it back in one piece? He stood again and started to pace.

CHAPTER SIX

It was twenty-two minutes before the Daydreamer casualties were sighted. His relief was only partial as he listened to the communications. It was decided that the helo would hover and the boat would make the rescue.

Once the boat arrived, Sam remained above until every boater had been brought aboard the Apalachee. Then she radioed they were heading back. He acknowledged and sat down again.

The lightning had stopped and the thunder could be heard in the distance. The patter of rain on the roof was back to a bearable volume, but he couldn't sit still. Until every member of the crew came back alive and unhurt, he'd wonder.

Finally, the sound of the rotors of the Dolphin announced its arrival. He was near the window of the glass radio room when the hangar doors opened. As the helo was pulled inside, he stepped to the doorway.

Emilio and Drew closed the hangar doors. Kolbe jumped off the Dolphin and Tyler could clearly see

Sam doing her final shut down. He breathed deeply. Rescue accomplished and everyone back safe.

But what about later in the shift? What about tomorrow? What about Wednesday when he had to go up in the helo for a patrol? He and Ryan needed to work faster.

Emilio bounded up the steps to see him. They had a friendly competition going.

"Tyler, you lucked out. I almost had four. That would have put me ahead of you by two."

He chuckled and moved back into the room, not comfortable so close to the top of the metal stairs. "It just wasn't your night." He sat in his chair again, more relaxed now that all were back safe. "How were the seas?"

"Rough. But Gonzalez had no problems. No one panicked."

"Too bad it's not always that way."

Emilio shrugged. "When people fear for their lives, they are bound to go a little loco. All part of the job."

He nodded. "Yeah. Glad it went well for everyone."

Emilio nodded. "Still made me hungry as a dogfish. You want anything from downstairs?"

"Sure."

"You got it." Emilio turned and exited the room.

Tyler turned back to his computer, listening to Emilio's footsteps head down the stairs. Then a loud noise broke in followed by shout and a loud clanging.

A female scream echoed in the hangar, and he ran to the door.

His whole body froze. The banister on the metal stairs was gone. He grasped the door tightly, knowing in his gut that Emilio had fallen onto the concrete below. Suddenly, his own fall, swamped his brain and he swayed.

"Tyler! Get down here! Sam, call 911." Kolbe's voice sounded confident, what they were all trained to be in the middle of a crisis.

He sucked in a deep breath and let it out slowly. He had to get down there. He was the most medically trained and Emilio's life depended on it.

Drew's voice floated up to him. "Should we roll him over? See if he landed on anything?"

Tyler forced himself to respond at that. "Don't touch him! I'm coming."

He took another deep breath and stepped onto the landing. Keeping his hand and his gaze to the wall on his right, he concentrated on taking one step at a time. Sweat beaded on his upper lip and his stomach protested his descent, but he made it to the bottom without another episode of his own fall flooding him.

Kolbe looked up from his crouched position next to a still Emilio. "Shit, took you long enough."

He strode forward, hoping the observant lieutenant wouldn't ask any questions as to why. No such luck.

"You sick or something, Tyler?"

He shook his head. "No, I was just doing a few push-ups to get the blood flowing. Sitting on my ass all shift sucks." As he spoke, he examined Emilio. The man was out cold, which was a good thing. "There's a good chance he broke either his neck or his back or both. Did you see how far up he was?"

Kolbe shook his head, but Drew pointed. "I did. He was only about three stairs down."

At least Emilio still breathed. He hoped to hell the man wasn't paralyzed. He had a wife and a baby on the way.

Anger, raw and edgy barreled through him. This had to stop. Glaring at each crew member, he gave them curt instructions as he treated Emilio for shock. He was ready to accuse every one of them of causing the fall, so he kept his instructions short.

Clenching his jaw, he checked his friend's pulse again.

"Will he live?" Drew's hesitant voice just infuriated him further. "Fuck if I know."

Kolbe's hand on his shoulder was meant to calm, but he was so far from that it took all his strength not to turn and punch the man. "Tyler, relax. The ambulance is on the way."

He gritted his teeth and didn't respond. When the ambulance finally arrived, he gave the EMT's Emilio's vitals then climbed in after him. He turned to face the crew. Sam, Drew, and Kolbe all looked worried. He ran his hand through his hair, not sure what to think. "Stay here and cover me. I'll call when I know something." He shut the doors.

As the ambulance raced away, he took out his phone. "Hey, Chief, we've had another accident."

Meghan leaned back in the chair next to the hospital bed. "So, did you call my sister?"

Alix nodded, her blond hair pulled back into a neat ponytail. She looked better, more color was in her cheeks. "Yes. We shared horror stories."

"And…."

"We're going to talk again. We both had some similar reactions. I like her."

Meghan smiled. "Good. I do too." She winked. "How's your dad handling everything?"

Alix rolled her eyes. "He's like a bull, running roughshod over everyone, yelling at them to get answers. Did I tell you he was once a Marine?"

"No, you didn't. How did he feel about you going into the Coast Guard?"

Alix laughed. "At first, he didn't want me near the service, but I signed up anyway. Then he railed against the Coast Guard saying his girl was good enough to be a Marine."

She could just imagine what it must have been

like for Alix's father. From what she understood, Alix was the only girl in the family and the youngest at that. She was one strong woman to stand up to her dad. "Has he ever come to terms with you being in the USCG?"

Alix shook her head. "Dad doesn't come to terms with anything until it's past. When I was top of my class in flight-school, he finally accepted my enrollment with the CG. He didn't want me stationed here because it was too far away, but then he was cool with me being a pilot. He's just never happy. You get used to it."

"Has he asked you to come home to recuperate?"

Alix looked away. "Yeah. He just doesn't get that I'm not going to get better."

Meghan's impulse was to tell the woman that she didn't know that for sure, but that was her personal reaction. She had to keep her comments related to helping Alix. "And did you agree to go home?"

She shook her head. "He'd just smother me. Feel sorry for me. I don't want to deal with that on top of this." She looked at her legs and frowned.

It was obvious she was trying to move them. Nothing happened.

"If you don't go home, what—"

A knock at the door interrupted her. She looked at Alix who shrugged. "It's not time for my physical therapy yet. Come in."

Meghan pulled her glasses down so she could identify who entered.

The door opened and a very haggard Tyler walked in. He was in his flight suit, but it was half unzipped revealing a tank beneath. His short hair stood up on end like he'd spent the night running his hand through it and his eyes were blood shot.

"Shit Tyler, you look like crap." Alix frowned.

His gaze moved from Alix to herself and he paused. "I'm sorry. I didn't know you were in a session. I'll come back."

"No wait." Her instinct told her he actually couldn't come back. Something important was on his mind. She may not be his therapist, but she considered herself his friend. "Come in. I can always stay later. Alix is my last appointment of the day."

He nodded. "Actually, I'm glad you're here."

"Come on Tyler, spill." Alix lifted her chin at him. "What's happened? And don't tell me another accident."

As he looked Alix in the eye, Meghan's heart skipped a beat. It couldn't be.

"You win the prize. Yay you." Tyler's expression was pure disgust.

"What the hell? Who? How? Are they okay?" Alix's eyes had grown wide and whether she knew it or not, she clasped the sheets with a death grip.

Tyler strode forward and sat in the chair on

the other side of the bed, obviously physically and emotionally exhausted. Meghan wanted to give him a hug.

"It's Emilio. We had a casualty last night and everyone came back in one piece, but then he was headed down the stairs from the radio room and the banister just fell off the fucking stairs. He must have been holding on to it or something and he went over."

"Oh, my God." Meghan couldn't help herself. "Is he okay?"

Tyler shook his head. "No. He's broken his back in three places."

"Jesus H. Christ." Alix's face lost all its color. "He's got a pregnant wife. Is he…is he…"

Her inability to say the words told Meghan volumes about where Alix was in her healing process and it wasn't very far. She helped her out because Tyler just frowned, probably too tired to catch on. "Is he paralyzed?"

He raised his eyebrows, obviously surprised by the question. "No. At least I don't think so. The doctors didn't say anything about that. They are keeping him immobile so that doesn't happen." He gave Alix a tired smile. "He's stable and on pain medication and his wife is with him now."

Alix's shoulders relaxed. "I'm glad. I wouldn't wish this on my worst enemy, never mind a friend."

Tyler shook his head. "This sucks."

Both Coast Guardsmen remained silent, so Meghan did as well. They obviously felt very close to Emilio. Her work kept her from making close bonds with others in her field or with her clients. She had a close bond with her sister before she'd gone to Afghanistan, but now they only spoke on the phone. It was as if her sister was afraid of her.

"Dr. Haskell, I know it's not 03:00 yet, but if you don't mind, I think I'm done for today."

"Of course." She stood, resisting the urge to give Alix a hug. "I will see you again on Friday."

"Thanks Doc."

"I'll walk out with you." Tyler rose from his chair, his body screaming tiredness but something else. Frustration? Anger? Both were to be expected.

He opened the door for her and ushered her out, his hand on the small of her back. She really liked the way he did that. They walked to the elevators in silence. But once there, she couldn't hold back any longer. She ached for him and wanted to do something. "When was the last time you ate?"

He looked at her blankly for a moment before answering. "I don't know. I guess last night's dinner before the Mayday."

She hooked her arm in his. "Then I'm taking you straight down to the cafeteria and buying you dinner."

He gave her a half-hearted smile. "Are you asking me on a date?"

She smiled, making it bright enough for both of them. "I guess I am."

The elevator doors opened, and she pressed the button marked Lower Level. Alix wasn't the first patient she'd visited at Westward Memorial and she probably wouldn't be the last, especially if the accidents at the Air Station continued.

She looked at Tyler out of the corner of her eye. His mind was definitely somewhere other than the elevator. When the elevator stopped on the second floor, he looked ready to get off. She grabbed his arm as they still had two floors to go.

A man in a sport coat and khakis walked in, his gray beard neatly trimmed but his hair in need of a cut.

"Dr. Preston. What are you doing here?" Tyler's knowledge of one of the other three psychologists in town surprised her.

Gerald Preston smiled. "Good to see you, Tyler. Hello, Dr. Haskell."

She nodded, preferring to let the two men talk.

He returned his attention to Tyler. "I just got off my shift in the psych ward. If you don't mind my saying, you don't look so good."

Tyler chuckled tiredly. "I've heard that a lot in the last hour. I haven't slept in over twenty-four. It was a rough night at the station."

"I'm sorry to hear that." The elevator doors

opened on the lobby level, cutting the conversation short. Dr. Preston strode out and they were left alone.

As the elevator continued to the lower level, she could feel Tyler's tension. As someone taking him on a "date," it was within her purview to ask why he knew Dr. Preston, but as a psychologist, and not Tyler's, she didn't want to pry.

When the doors opened, he let her exit first and it dawned on her how lucky she was that Tyler never *had* come to see her after his accident. If he had, what they were doing right now could cause her to lose her license, even go to jail.

She looked over the food choices and ordered a cheeseburger then made herself a salad from the salad bar. "Where would you like to sit?"

Tyler piled macaroni and cheese on to his second plate. "Wherever you like."

She took her food up to the register. "I'll be paying for that man over there." She handed the cashier her credit card.

The lady winked. "I'd pay for him, too."

She smiled in return. "I'll be right back. Don't let him pay. I just want to put my tray down." She walked over to a quiet corner. Since it was mid-afternoon, there weren't many people in the cafeteria. The few who were, looked as stressed as Tyler.

She set her food on the table and lifted her tray to bring it to the window.

"Dr. Haskell. Have you come to see Emilio?"

She started as Drew strode toward her. She felt guilty which made no sense. Drew was a patient, Tyler wasn't. "No, I'm not. I just finished with Alix. Why? Do you think Emilio will want to talk to me?"

Drew leaned his hip against another table. "I have no idea. I just got off and was headed up to see him. Thought I'd grab a pop first."

She smiled kindly. "That's nice of you. I don't know if he's up for visitors, but I'm sure the doctor will let you know."

"How did you find out? Did the chief call you?" Drew's eye lit with interest. How odd. "No, I was in with Alix when Tyler came by to tell her."

"Oh."

"Hey kid. You aren't making a move on my date, now are you?" Tyler placed his tray on the table.

Drew stiffened. She knew how much he hated being called "kid." "Date? You two are dating?"

She laughed. "If me buying Tyler a meal in a hospital cafeteria is a date, then I guess the answer is 'yes'."

Tyler gave her a tired smile. "You really didn't have to do that, Meghan."

At the sound of her name in his voice, she melted. Crap, she really had it bad for him. She lifted her glasses up on top of her head and gazed into his gray eyes.

"Well, I'm going to see how Emilio is doing."

Drew's tone was accusatory, as if neither of them cared.

Tyler's jaw tightened. "If he's asleep, don't bother him. He's on pain killers."

"I bet he is." Drew turned to go then stopped. "By the way Tyler, if you're going to go on a date, the least you could do is change. See you Thursday, Dr. Haskell."

Meghan laid her hand over Tyler's fisted one. "He's only twenty-one."

"Right." He opened his hand and caught hers. "Thank you for the meal and the company."

She felt her cheeks heat. "It's the least I can do. I'm sorry about Emilio. I didn't have the government contract last year. Is this a normal number of occurrences?"

Tyler let go of her hand and picked up his fork. "No."

When he didn't say anything else, she took the opportunity to get her credit card from the cashier. When she turned back, Tyler was watching her. A little un-nerved, she couldn't help remember the encounter with Dr. Preston. Was Tyler seeing him for something? Preston was known for counselling those with anger issues. Was Tyler too good to be true because there was another side?

When she sat down, she noticed he hadn't started eating. "Is everything okay?"

"It's great. I just didn't want to start without you." He gave her that tired grin again.

The man was politeness to the core. "I'm sorry. Please go ahead."

He still waited until her fork had speared her salad before he dove into his meal. Actually, it was two meals. The poor man was starved.

They ate in companionable silence and when she finished her food, she sat back and watched him.

Tyler was an enigma. He was psychologically strong enough not to need to see her after his accident, but as soon as one of his friends was hurt, he became emotional and protective. She admired that. His loyalty and honor was impeccable.

So why did he know Dr. Preston? *Meg just ask him. Otherwise it's going to drive you crazy.* If Tyler didn't know her profession, she might, but asking that kind of question was borderline unethical and she just wouldn't go there.

When he finished, he sat back and wiped his mouth with the napkin he'd put on his lap. "I needed that. Thank you again."

"It was my pleasure. I didn't realize a man could consume so much in one sitting."

He laughed. "You have obviously not been on base during lunchtime. They make us certain dishes to be sure we get enough calories. Our adrenaline while on the job uses a ton. I've been running on fumes for hours."

"I'm glad I could help. Is there anything else I can do?"

Tyler's eyes darkened as he studied her, making her heart race. "Actually, there is."

Oh God, did he want to kiss her? If so, she was all for it. She dropped her gaze to his lips.

"I came here in the ambulance with Emilio. Any chance you could give me a ride home? I could ask Drew, but I don't feel like dealing with him right now." He gave her a shrug.

A ride? "Yes. I mean, of course. I'd be happy to."

"Are you sure? I could call a cab. I live a little out of the way."

She placed her hand on his again. "Tyler, I'd be happy to. I haven't had the day you've had and with no other clients and only notes to do when I get home, I welcome the side trip." She smiled, more than happy to help.

"Thank you." He stood and reached his hand down to her.

He was such a gentleman. Taking his hand, she rose expecting them to walk out, but instead he pulled her to him and his other arm wrapped around her waist. Every nerve ending woke up.

"I'd like to reciprocate. Will you have dinner with me tomorrow night?"

It was hard to focus on his words when her body touched his in many places and his face was so close. "Yes. I'd like that."

"I know a great seafood place called Ruby's on the River. Do you like seafood?"

She nodded. Her mouth having gone dry at the darkening of his eyes to a tar gray.

They stood nose to nose for at least a minute when he suddenly released her. She felt as if someone had thrown a bucket of ice water over her. Disappointment at not receiving what had appeared would be a kiss, had her feeling awkward. "Uh, my car is in the visitor's lot."

He nodded. "Unfortunately, I know that lot well." Holding his arm out, he let her precede him.

CHAPTER SEVEN

As Meghan drove Tyler home, they talked about what most new friends talk about. Where they grew up, him in Maine and herself in New Jersey, what they liked to do when not working, their jobs.

As she turned down a dirt road at his direction, she started to feel uneasy. Each side of the road was Florida swamp, complete with Spanish moss on old cedar trees. It was the perfect place for an abduction.

She glanced at Tyler who watched the road. "Do you ever see alligators out here?"

"Many times. But I also see opossums, armadillos, racoons, ospreys, hawks, and Bald Eagles. That's why I live so far off the beaten path. Take this left."

She slowed the car down to turn. "Okay, I would not have thought this was a road."

He chuckled. "It's not. It's my driveway."

She continued slowly because her undercarriage was obviously lower than his truck and the weeds in the middle of the "driveway" were a little high. When they came around a curve, a small house on a manmade hill came into view, and she slowed. "How perfect. Is it yours?"

"No, I rent it. Moving to a new station every two to three years, makes owning a house a pain, though if I find a place I really like, I hope to buy it and keep it for retirement."

"You're in the right state for that." She brought the vehicle to a stop and stared. The driveway came up alongside the house. It was close to six and the sun had just started to set on the Gulf. The back of the house looked out on that wide expanse of water. "Wow."

He exited the vehicle and opened the driver side door. "Come. I see this every night I don't work. I rarely get to share it." He bent his arm, and she hooked hers through it then they moved slowly as she picked her steps carefully. Her high heel pumps were not made for the jungle-like environment while his Coast Guard boots were perfect.

When they reached the back, he led her to a patio with a table and four chairs. "Have a seat. You won't want to miss this. I'll get us a drink. I only have the tea I bought with you the other day, but I also have beer and wine."

A golden glow from the sun lit his hair, making it a lighter blond than it already was. It also made his eyes appear lighter. "I'll have a beer."

He nodded then went around to the side door.

She glanced at the area. She was definitely taking her chances. The house was incredibly isolated. But knowing what she did of Tyler, she felt oddly safe. The question was, did what Dr. Preston know about Tyler, put her in danger? Was Tyler seeing the doctor for anger management or was it something benign like the loss of a loved one? Maybe it was simply that the two had met at a function.

The sliding glass door behind her opened, so she turned.

Tyler had taken off his flight suit, leaving him in shorts and a tank. She'd never been fond of tanks on men, but on Tyler it looked amazing, showing off the muscles from his shoulders to his forearms and the man had muscles. That made sense since he was a rescue swimmer.

He handed her the beer. She smiled as he poured it in a frosty mug, though he drank from a bottle.

"Please sit and enjoy the show." His grin was a bit less tired. The food must have helped.

She set her mug on the table and pulled out a chair. Tyler picked up one of the iron chairs with padding in one hand and brought it around to set it next to her. He held up his bottle "Cheers."

She lifted hers. "To a beautiful sunset."

"And a beautiful woman." He clinked his bottle to her mug before she could protest and took a swig."

Her cheeks filled with heat. She'd never blushed

so much around a man before. It had to be that he always caught her off guard with his compliments.

The sun had hit some low-lying clouds and the color started to change. "How did you find this place?"

He shrugged, the muscles in his shoulders looking bigger as he did it. "I lucked out. I came a couple weeks early and scoped out the area. Every duty station offers different advantages. It doesn't take a genius to recognize the best part about being in the boonies of north-central Florida is the wildlife."

"They do call this the Nature Coast."

He laughed. "True. But touristy slogans can't always be trusted."

She nodded, but didn't look at him, her gaze riveted to the kaleidoscope of yellows, oranges and reds in the sky. "If I lived here, I'd be home before sunset every single day." When he didn't respond, she looked at him, raising her glasses to the top of her head.

If she thought the scenery in the sky was mesmerizing, Tyler in his relaxed state looking at her with desire darkened eyes was a whole other ballgame.

"Do you know your skin is glowing?" He stared at her lips.

She shook her head, but watched him as her breaths became shallow.

"It is. You are impossible to resist." His hand came around her neck and he pulled her face closer to his. He held her there as if waiting for her to pull away or tell him to stop. Hell would have to freeze over for that to happen.

When she did neither, he finally pulled her in for a kiss. Her body electrified at the touch of his lips upon hers, but as he nudged her mouth open and swept his tongue inside, she melted against him.

She grasped his waist, feeling the movement of muscle beneath her hand, even as he leaned forward and wrapped his other arm around her to pull her flush against him. Her breasts were crushed against the hard planes of his chest, causing sparks to ignite inside her. She sighed as he dominated her mouth and his hand grasped her ass to pull her closer.

But they were twisted, and no matter how much they wanted it, they would have to move.

He lifted his mouth away from hers and kissed her neck once before leaning his forehead against hers. "You're missing the sunset."

"I've seen sunsets before. I've never felt quite like this before though."

He sighed and let her go.

Crap, what did she say? *Come back.*

He ran his hand through his hair. "I need to shower and to get some sleep. I have an early shift tomorrow and as much as I would love to spend the evening with you, I've been up over twenty-four hours and doubt I could stay awake."

Of course. What an idiot she was. "That's right. You've had a rough couple of days." She stood, suddenly embarrassed by her lack of observation. She was usually more attuned to others than that. She'd been selfish. "I should head home."

He stood and opened his arm toward the driveway. "We're still on for tomorrow night, right?"

She smiled. "Yes. I'm looking forward to it."

He opened the car door for her and she slipped inside.

"Wait, how will you get to the station tomorrow?"

He pointed to a detached garage. "My Harley. I'll just roll it up into the bed of the truck and bring it home when I get off."

A part of her was hoping he'd need a ride, but that would be pushing herself on him.

He handed her his phone. "Mind putting your number and address in here. My eyes are so blurry I'm pretty sure I'd mess it up."

Her heart fluttered which was silly. It was just a number and address. Nothing more. Still, she double checked to make sure she'd entered everything correctly. "Here you go."

He took his phone back and stuffed it in his pocket. "How's 18:00? I can pick you up then."

She counted in her head. Six o'clock. "That's perfect."

"Great." He leaned over and kissed her again. Just a good night kiss on the lips. Then he closed her door and backed away from the car.

She waved, then backed her sedan around, turned on her headlights, and headed back toward civilization, feeling more excited than she had since getting her first kiss when she was fifteen.

Tyler was one in a million. She couldn't believe some lucky lady hadn't claimed him yet. Her spirits lowered as she turned onto a paved road again. Did the reason Tyler wasn't taken have something to do with him knowing Dr. Preston?

Tyler pulled up to his house to find Ryan's white pick-up in front. Jumping out, he strode around back to see if Ryan was waiting on the patio, but he wasn't there. If Ryan was here, it meant he'd been able to call in another favor.

Striding around to the side door, he felt adrenaline pumping at their potential success. He unlocked his door and stopped. "How did you get in here?"

Ryan looked up from the dining room table and grinned. "Good to see you, too. As for getting in, your slider was unlocked."

Shit, he really had been tired last night if he'd forgotten to lock that. He was slipping. His father would be up one side of him and down the other if he ever heard of such a stupid move. "I'm glad to see you. Does this mean you have some more info?"

Ryan faced him, leaning his ass against the table. "I do. It's not enough to figure out who is behind everything, but it will help."

Tyler threw his keys on the end table in the living room and strode toward Ryan. "What did you get?"

Ryan picked up a packet of papers. "The preliminary findings on Alix's accident."

Tyler grabbed them out of Ryan's hand and pulled out a chair. Scanning the single-spaced document, he finally looked up. "Put this in laymen's terms for me, will you?"

Ryan sat too. "Sure. It was really simple. It was a loose bolt in the tail shaft that caused the tail rotor to stop working."

"How could there be a loose bolt?"

Ryan shook his head. "There can't. Someone glued it to the side. It didn't take long for the glue to let go and bang, dead tail rotor."

Tyler found himself crunching the papers in his hand and he quickly dropped them on the table. "How long would it take. I mean, was this something that might last a few flights, or would it only last through a partial flight."

"With the spin of that rotor, I'm surprised it didn't let go before the Dolphin cleared the base."

"Fuck." Tyler stood, his blood pumping too hard

to sit. "That means whoever did this wasn't on Alix's flight. That leaves my crew. Great. I'm back on regular duty in two days. In the meantime, our sister station down south is going to cover us."

"What about your other rescue swimmer?"

"We had another 'accident'."

"Damn, he isn't…?"

"No, but he'll be laid up for months."

"Actually, that might help us." Ryan pulled a pad from next to a winch and flipped the top page over, which had a sketch of what looked like a tail rotor. "Tell me what happened."

He explained Emilio's fall and answered all Ryan's questions. "What are you thinking?"

"I'm thinking the traitor is getting pretty bold."

He nodded. He'd thought that as well. "I was hoping to pin this on Drew as he's a mechanic, but with the stairs, the ceiling joist and the stored equipment, it doesn't take a mechanic to figure out how to make those events happen. Besides, Drew was hurt in one of those."

"Let me get this straight. Your crew is you, Kolbe, Sam and Drew, correct?"

"Yes." He watched as Ryan wrote down the names.

"If we get rid of Drew and yourself. That leaves Sam and Kolbe."

Ryan ran his hand through his hair. "But to cut my cable with a ratcheting cable cutter, they would have to climb out of the pilot seat. There's no way to do that without Drew seeing something."

Ryan pondered that. "Well, the answer to that is not good."

He sat back down, defeated despite all the evidence. "Yeah, either someone set up my cable ahead of time and got lucky, or we have two people working together and if that's the case then Drew is back in the mix."

Ryan nodded.

He wanted to hit something, anything. "The only consolation is that the investigators know someone is causing these mishaps."

"No, all they know is that yours and Alix's were caused by someone. The other injuries will probably be deemed as caused by accidents."

He stared at the table as Ryan doodled on his pad. His return to duty put all the crews in jeopardy if he and Ryan couldn't find the culprit. "Hey, thanks for helping out on this. I know I'm taking you away from what you love to work on."

Ryan grinned. "You mean horses and engines?"

He nodded.

"It's not a problem. Neither my horses nor my machines are in yet, so the only work I'm missing out on is carpentry and paint. I hate that. Really, glad Lynzie is handling the house stuff."

"And your two buddies there are filling in for you?"

"Yup. Jessie Reynolds and Cooper Maddox. You met them when I gave you the tour."

"Right." He got up and strode to the fridge. "You need anything?"

"No, I helped myself earlier."

Tyler grabbed a can of iced tea and leaned against the door way. "At least I can bring this to the chief. Right now, he thinks I'm as crazy as Kolbe with his voodoo stuff."

Ryan shook his head. "No, you can't. This hasn't been released yet. It probably won't hit your station for another week."

He swallowed the tea in his mouth quickly. "We could all be dead by then."

Ryan frowned. "You still have three possibles, Kolbe, Sam and Drew. Drew was hurt, but that could be a good cover. Maybe you can get your psychologist friend to talk."

At the thought of Meghan, he looked at his watch. He needed to shower soon. "I tried that already. Didn't get anywhere."

"What about taking her into your confidence?"

Just going to dinner was risking a lot. At least by choosing Ruby's, he knew they wouldn't be high up. The place was right at ground level. He took another swig of tea then answered. "I guess I have to. We have no other leads. I'm taking her out to dinner tonight."

"Hah! I was right. You *do* like her." Ryan grinned.

Since the man had finally married his high school sweetheart, he seemed to think every man needed a 'good woman by his side', as he put it.

"What's not to like? She's smart, thoughtful, kind and beautiful. Can't blame me for trying." Can only blame me for hiding my stupid fear.

"Okay, you tackle that end," Ryan winked at his double entendre, "and if you want, I can come to the station with you tomorrow and take a look at that railing. Have they replaced it yet?"

"No, but they are supposed to tomorrow afternoon. I work in the morning."

"Guess you don't plan on a late night then. Too bad." Ryan's fake frown was too much.

Tyler shook his head. "I need to shower. Feel free to let yourself out."

"Sure. I let myself in, didn't I?" Ryan's chuckle followed him all the way to the bathroom.

Ryan's cheery outlook could get on his nerves, but he couldn't have discovered this much without him. Maybe he could get a tune up for his bike when Ryan was done at the station tomorrow. After all, the guy seemed to miss his engines.

CHAPTER EIGHT

Meghan took off the short black dress and rehung it. It looked great, but it was so typical. She was always conservative. She wanted Tyler Adams in her life. She just needed to encourage him a bit more.

His kisses were to die for and his body had her hearing angels, but his personality made her heart fill with happiness. She could see a real relationship with him. Now she wanted to take it further.

Returning to her walk-in closet, she ignored her suits and focused on her dresses. Her sundresses were pretty pastels, but she'd heard about Ruby's on the River, and it was expensive. She still couldn't believe Tyler wanted to take her there. That had to be a good thing. A red spaghetti strap cling dress caught her eye, but it was just a little too bold for her.

Pushing that one aside, she found one. It was purple, tight but instead of spaghetti straps it had a halter with a collar look and fell just above her knees. Perfect. Slipping into it, she decided on lavender strappy high heels, amethyst earrings and a lavender clutch purse.

Glancing at the clock, she pulled out a lavender shawl with pansies printed on it and headed for her living room. Her two-bedroom house on two acres was the opposite direction of Tyler's. She was much farther inland on high and dry land. No alligators. Just lawn, tall grasses and the neighbor's house not too far away.

The sound of a truck pulling into her driveway sent her heart into double time. She checked her hair one more time. She arranged it in a loose bun with a few wisps out to frame her face. Would he like how she looked? Crap, she was acting like a teenager. She had her doctorate degree for crying out loud. *Grow up.*

Yeah, she could be calm and collected, but the butterflies in her stomach felt good. She didn't remember the last time she was this excited to see a man. She waited at the archway between her kitchen and living room for the inevitable knock. Throwing the door open before Tyler even made it to the steps, would make her appear over anxious, which she was.

At the sound of his footsteps on her porch, she started across the room. His knock sounded as she reached the door. She should count to twenty, but she only made it to ten before she opened it.

Wow. Tyler wore a navy-blue suit that fit him perfectly, making his broad shoulders stand out. His blue shirt and red and blue patterned tie completed his look.

She finally smiled and released her breath. "You clean up beautifully."

"Me? You look amazing. Of course, you always do." His admiration was obvious, and she felt her cheeks heat.

"Just let me get my shawl and purse." She turned around, and walked back into her kitchen where she'd laid both items down. When she turned back to face him, she caught him looking at her butt. Her whole body heated at his look.

Polite as always, he raised his gaze quickly. "Is this your house?"

"Yes. I bought it about a year ago. I didn't want to be too far from town, but I did want a little space in case I decided to do some gardening."

"And have you?"

She laughed. "Not yet. Maybe when I retire I'll have the time."

He raised his eyebrows. "Retire? You sound like me, planning for the future. Actually, this is exactly what I was thinking. If I could find a place like this, I'd buy it."

That he liked her house so much, or what he saw of it, pleased her. How silly. This was only their first official date, though to be fair, they'd had a couple others and she'd spoken with him many other times.

"Are you ready?" He held out his arm.

"I am. I've never been to Ruby's. I can't wait to try it." She hooked her arm in his, and he walked her to her door, before stepping back and allowing her to exit first. Then he locked the door from inside and pulled it shut. "Do you have a dead bolt?"

She shook her head. "Do you think I need one?"

He examined the surrounding area. "In the daylight, you are in view of your neighbors, but at night there is less chance of them seeing anyone in your yard. It couldn't hurt to have one installed."

She'd never thought of that. Most of her neighbors were retired, so she hadn't been concerned about them, but that didn't mean others couldn't come into the area and take advantage of what they thought was all elderly residents. "Thank you. I think I will. Do you always think about safety?"

He grinned sheepishly. "Can't help it. It's in my blood."

He opened his truck passenger door and helped her in. She noticed his gaze flick to her thigh as her dress rode up a bit as she sat down. Knowing he was interested, helped her to relax. She didn't want a one-way relationship like her last one.

As he drove them to the restaurant, she learned that he'd never been there either, which made her feel special. He'd only been in town for eight months and was scheduled for a two-year stint. He could pick his preferred next stops, but he didn't always get them. He'd have better luck if he got the promotion he put in for.

She told him about her move to Florida and how excited her parents were that they would have a place to come in the winter, and had availed themselves of her home every year. It was why she bought a two-bedroom house.

When they arrived at the restaurant, he led her to the door, his hand on the small of her back, which sent tingles racing up her spine. He was seriously more than she'd dreamed of in a man. As they walked in, she wasn't oblivious to the looks Tyler received from the women, young and old alike. She was so proud to be with him.

After being seated and ordering, she smiled at him, anxious to learn more about him. "You said you used to fight with your brothers. How many do you have?"

"I have three. One's a Maine Game Warden, another is a State Trooper, and the other is still deciding what he wants to be when he grows up. We are hoping he'll get into law enforcement or the military, but I don't think that will happen."

"Why?"

Tyler smirked. "Let's just say, he's different. He never hunts or fishes like ninety-percent of the population and he loves school." Tyler grimaced.

As an excellent student, she had loved school too. "How old is he?"

"He's twenty. We're all four years apart. My mom said it took her that long to get us trained right."

"I think I like your mom." She smiled. Anyone who could produce such a gentleman had to be special.

He studied her for a moment. "I think she'd like you too. She's anxious to have daughters-in-law. None of us are married. Not even my older brother."

She nodded. "That's to be expected. In my studies, I learned a lot about birth-order and parents of single sex children. It helped me understand my own mother."

"Don't tell me there are more beautiful Haskell women running around out there."

"You are certainly laying on the charm." She smiled to be sure he knew she enjoyed it.

"Is it working?"

She pretended to ponder. "I think it is."

The waitress returned with their meal. He'd ordered the trout and she had the shrimp. All seafood served at Ruby's was caught that day in the rivers that ran into the Gulf or in the Gulf itself. There were many places to eat that boasted the same freshness, but most were t-shirt and short places, where people stopped for food after or during a day on the water.

She took a bite and closed her eyes. It was that

good. When she opened them, she found Tyler staring at her, his fork halfway to his mouth, his eyes dark.

"When you do that, you make me want to kiss you." His voice was low and husky.

Her heart skipped over a beat. "I like that."

He gave her a devilish grin that had her whole body revving. "I mean kiss you *all* over."

She grabbed her glass of wine and gulped. He wasn't usually so bold. It made her want to skip dinner all together and go back to her place. She took a deep breath before responding. "What's good for the goose should be good for the gander."

He stopped chewing. His gaze went from her eyes to her breasts and back. "I agree."

She coughed and quickly looked away. She'd never get through the meal if they kept that up. She already knew what she wanted for dessert. Him.

"You said you have sisters?"

Thank you. She needed to get her mind out of bed and talking about Jessie would do it. "Only one. She's younger and lives here in Florida too, but she's staying with a friend. She was wounded in Afghanistan."

Tyler dropped his grin immediately and gave her his total attention. "I'm sorry, but glad she made it out alive. I lost a number of friends over there. The problem with that country is that it can happen anytime. There's no front, per se. My friend Ryan, who you met, is a mechanic and he caught a bullet in the hip while working on an Abrams tank."

She stilled. "You served over there?"

He nodded. "Most civilians don't realize that the Coast Guard does work overseas. We have particular specialties that other branches don't. That's how I met Ryan."

"He's the man you brought over to the hangar that day, right? My sister is staying at a Ryan's farm. This man is going to use a horse farm to help rehabilitate veterans who have physical and emotional scars."

He put down his fork. "That's my friend. Your sister is living there? Is her name Jessie?"

"Yes." She couldn't keep the excitement from her voice. To have another connection with Tyler had to mean this was right.

"I met a Jessie there, but her last name wasn't Haskell."

She shook her head. "Reynolds was her married name."

"Was?"

"She had one of those two month marriages. Luckily, she realized the guy wasn't right for her and got out before they bought a house or had kids. She's a lot more spontaneous than I am."

Tyler wiped his mouth with his napkin and picked up his wine glass. "I propose a toast to the Haskell sisters."

She raised her glass, curious.

"To their success in life."

She clinked her glass with his and smiled. If she had any doubts, even those about him possibly seeing Dr. Preston, they were washed away. This man was the real deal.

The waitress came back to clear their plates and offer dessert. They both turned it down. Tyler's wink made it clear they were thinking the same thing.

He leaned forward and took her hand. "I have an important question for you."

"Ask away."

His face said it was serious. "Do you think Alix might have a fear of heights after her accident?"

Huh, where did that come from? "Why would she have that?"

He shrugged. "I don't know. Maybe because her Dolphin went down?"

She pulled her hand away as her libido cooled and her professional thoughts took over. "I couldn't say either way. She's one of my patients and that entitles her to doctor-patient confidentiality."

He frowned and warning bells started to sound. Did he like Alix too?

"That means you can't tell me anything about Drew or Leo or Steve either because of this confidentiality?"

Her heart slowed down considerably. She didn't like where this was going or where her thoughts were headed. "No. It's against the law, not to mention unethical. *Any* psychologist is bound by that. Only a court subpoena could make me turn over my notes or make me reveal anything about any of my patients. Why do you ask?"

Tyler ran his hand through his hair for the first time that night, which put her further on edge. "I need your help, your insight."

He paused. Clearly, whatever he wanted to say, he didn't like revealing to her.

That in itself upset her. "Okay. About what?"

His gaze, which had wandered away from her, came back. "About the accidents at the Air Station. I've discovered that they all haven't been accidental."

She tensed. "What do you mean? That someone caused them?"

He nodded. "If I can't figure out who it is by 07:00 on Thursday, someone may get hurt."

She tried to wrap her brain around what he said, but it was almost too horrible to contemplate. "Why would someone want to hurt the air crews of Crystal Waters?"

"I don't have a clue. I thought maybe you could help."

"How could I help? I haven't even met them all." He wasn't making sense.

He leaned forward. "We are pretty sure that it's one of the crew members from my crew, so Sam, Kolbe or Drew. You've seen Drew, so maybe you could let us know if it's possible."

Oh God, he *did* want her to break the law. "You said 'we.' Who's 'we'?" Maybe the Coast Guard had asked him to ask for her help. She could explain it to them.

"Ryan and myself. If you think it could be Drew based on what you've seen, then we can find a way to keep him off the Dolphin until we can prove it. If you don't think it's him then we can focus on Kolbe and Sam."

She opened her mouth, but couldn't get her vocal chords to work. She was stunned. She should have known Tyler was too perfect. How could he ask her to do this? Wait, was this his motivation for asking her out?

Her heart felt like it shrunk inside her chest as a burn started in the pit of her stomach. "What does the Coast Guard say about all this."

"The investigators think that only the Dolphin accidents were sabotage, but I know the hangar accidents were too." Tyler scowled. "You have to help us or someone could get killed."

She'd heard enough. Standing, she kept her composure despite the hurt inside. "I can't help you. Please take me home now."

Tyler's gaze left her and scanned the room before he rose. "Of course." As he walked behind her, she hoped he wouldn't touch her. She wanted to vomit and that might just put her over the edge. She'd been a fool and now she would pay for it.

The moment Meghan stood, Tyler's stomach fell. Fuck. He'd been so focused on saving his crew, he stepped over the line with the woman he was falling for.

As they walked out, she appeared calm, but he could see the tension in her beautiful neck and in the grasp she had on her purse. Not only had he failed to figure out if Drew should be a suspect, but he'd pissed her off and he couldn't blame her. He'd be pissed too if someone asked him to break the law.

He opened the truck door for her and she climbed in. She remained poised but he could practically feel the anger radiating from her.

Once he joined her and headed down the road, he tried to find something to say that might ease her tension. It all sounded dumb to him, but he had to try. "I'm sorry if I offended you. I didn't mean to. I wasn't aware of the restrictions on your profession."

She didn't say a word.

"I can't stand to see my fellow crew members in danger. We are grounded for one more day then we go up again and all of us, except the person responsible will be in danger of losing our lives. I got carried away because of that. I hope you will forgive me."

She still didn't say anything.

He'd really screwed up this time. Even at the idea that she may not want to see him again, his heart constricted. Shit, he had it worse for Meghan than he realized. He had to find a way to make it right.

He pulled up to her house and got out to open her door, but she had already jumped down and pulled her dress lower. That was not a good sign. He walked her to the door, but didn't touch her. Everything about her shouted for him to keep his distance. He could do that for now, but he wanted Meghan Haskell in his life…however long that might be.

"Thank you, for dinner." Her words were polite and said without feeling.

Frustrated, he moved his hand through his hair. "I know you're mad at me. I understand, but I hope you will forgive my stupidity. I'd really like to see you again."

She didn't say anything. Instead, she opened her purse and took out her keys.

He placed his hand on her arm as she put the key in the lock. "After tomorrow, my life will be in danger. My hope is that I will live long enough to figure this out and see you again."

The only sign she gave that she heard him was her quick intake of breath. Then she turned the knob and walked into her home, turning the lock in the door as soon as it was shut.

Well, that wasn't how he'd expected the evening to end. Fuck.

———

Meghan poured hot water over her ginger-lemon tea before walking back to her desk to check her next appointment.

9:00 DREW LINDEN.

Quickly, she glanced outside. It was sunny, so no chance she'd run into Tyler. She hadn't heard from him since their date. She didn't want to either. She'd cried herself to sleep that night calling herself all kinds of fools.

She was more sure than ever that the only reason he had asked her to dinner was to get her to help him. She'd promised herself she wouldn't think about it, but she couldn't help it.

And the thought of Kolbe or Drew wanting to harm their own crew members, made her sick. She didn't know Samantha, but if she was anything like Alix then she wasn't responsible either. How did Tyler know it was a crew member? Maybe someone from outside had done it or even one of the boat crew members. She could think of all kinds of motivation from that angle.

What she couldn't understand is why Tyler went to so much trouble to get her to violate her code of ethics after he learned her clients were entitled to confidentiality? What kept her anger going was that he had taken her out on false pretenses and then even after hearing that it was illegal for her to divulge anything about any of her clients, he kept pressing her.

She moved back to her cabinet and took her teabag out. Adding some sugar, she stirred before taking her tea cup and going back to her desk. Though his apologies on the way home sounded sincere, if she meant anything to him, he would have contacted her by now. His lack of contact proved he had no real interest, unless…

She paused, about to take a sip of tea. *Unless he died in an accident yesterday.* Her heart froze. What if he had, or did, and she didn't do anything to help prevent it? Could she live with herself? *Crap.*

The receptionist's laugh outside clued her in to the fact that Drew must have arrived. That young woman loved to talk about Drew, but so far, he hadn't asked her out. Meghan took a sip of tea then set her cup down and strode to her door. She couldn't help her need to know that Tyler was all right.

When she opened the door, Drew looked up as if caught doing something he shouldn't. "I'm not late yet."

She smiled. "No, you aren't. I was just checking to see which man was making my receptionist giggle so much."

Drew bowed. "Me, of course." He looked at the

receptionist and winked before walking toward her. "I'm ready if you are."

She backed into her office and let him come in. After closing the door, she took her tea cup from the desk to the winged back chair she always sat in and took her glasses off.

Drew was already lying on the couch she had opposite the two large chairs. He was the only man who availed himself of that piece of furniture.

"You must have ridden your bike over since it's sunny."

He squinted his eyes at her. "Yes, I did. Why bother Tyler if I don't have to? Heard you two went on a date the other night."

She waved her hand, relieved to know that Tyler must still be alive based on how Drew phrased the question. "We did, but we're here to talk about you. I'm completely focused on you. How was your week since I last saw you?"

"The usual. They keep calling me 'kid' and giving me the crap jobs. Did Tyler talk about me on your date?"

She frowned, ignoring his question. "Giving you the 'crap' jobs doesn't seem fair unless you are the low man on the totem pole, so to speak. Do they all out-rank you?"

"Yeah, but that doesn't mean they can't help out with the boring stuff. I have to keep those helicopters in the air."

The investigators think that only the Dolphin accidents were sabotage… Tyler's words flitted through her head. Now she wished he'd never told her. Besides, Drew had been hurt as well. "Doesn't Steve help with that. He's another mechanic, right?"

"Yeah, he helps, but I'm a much better mechanic. I know what makes those birds tick. Did Tyler say Steve was a better mechanic?"

She gave Drew her best school-teacher look. "Drew, I was on a date. When I'm on a date, I talk about the person I'm with. We were getting to know each other."

"Sorry." He appeared sincere, so she continued.

"Maybe they make you do the 'crap' jobs because when they were your rank, they had to do them. I'm sure once you've been in longer, you'll have the chance to assign those tasks to the newbies."

He shook his head, his frown deepening. "I wish. I was up for promotion between my last assignment and this one. They totally screwed me." He looked slyly at her. "Not like your boyfriend who got a promotion before he came here and is now already up for another one. He'll probably get it too, despite being useless for four months."

There was so much resentment in Drew's voice that she cringed inwardly. While he didn't actually like any of his fellow Coast Guardsmen, she'd never heard him have that much animosity toward one. She didn't encourage it. "He's not my boyfriend. We just went on one date."

Drew sat up, his gaze never leaving her face. "But you like him, don't you?"

"Yes, I do. But I like you, too. Now let's keep the focus on you. Are the helicopters back in the air now? What was the last mission like?"

Luckily, that redirected Drew nicely as he complained about every slight, real or imagined.

"You say you're here for another eight months and it doesn't sound like the crew's attitude toward you is going to change, though I still believe they wouldn't joke with you if they didn't like you."

"They don't like me, except when I'm sweeping out the hangar."

She reminded herself of how young Drew was and kept the mothering tone out of her voice. "Whichever way it is, it is time for us to come up with another way for you to react toward the treatment."

That got his attention. "Like what?"

"That mainly depends on you. You say they are bullying. What do you do when they do that? Do you give it right back or do you cower?"

He frowned. "I can never think of something to say fast enough. It's only after they walk away that I think of something."

That gave her an idea. "Let's start with nicknames." She rose and walked over to her desk then came back with a pad of paper in her hand. "Here, write down everyone's name and then come up with a nickname for them. They call you 'kid' which is both affectionate and derogatory. Try to find the same balance with your names."

Drew's eyes lit with excitement. She handed him a pen and he started writing immediately.

She watched him as she sipped her tea. Could the "kid" really be the cause of the accidents? Sure, he resented the others, but it was more a self-pity then an actual anger. Similar to a teenager. Then again, teenagers had been known to do some pretty awful things to their peers, like shooting them. But they had serious mental issues. She didn't see Drew in that category.

She watched the time as Drew wrote and scratched out and wrote more. When their session was over, she put down her tea cup. "I'm afraid that's all our time for today. Why don't you give me the paper and you can continue with this first thing when you come back next week."

He nodded. "Yes. Maybe I'll think of more names by then." He smiled. "Thank you, Dr. Haskell. I think we're finally making real progress now."

What a perfect backward compliment. She smiled despite the dig and walked him out. She heard him start a conversation with the receptionist and sighed. She was pretty sure he just needed to grow up a bit more.

Dropping the pad of paper on her desk, she went back to her cabinet and started her electric kettle. Once it was ready, she poured water over an orange-cinnamon tea bag then moved to her desk to check her next appointment while it steeped. A phrase on the pad of paper next to her computer jumped out at her.

ACCIDENT WAITING TO HAPPEN

CHAPTER NINE

Meghan froze. What? She picked up the pad Drew had been writing on. He'd listed all the crew members on the left side and added names to the right of them. The first names were typical—Shorty, Bear, Diva, Bubba, Chica, Bro, Dude. But the next set were meaner—Jerk, Ho, Bitch face, Dickhead, Ass Wipe, Cocksucker, Pissant. It was the final set that he hadn't finished that alarmed her. Border Hopper, Ghetto, Cunt, Deadman and the one that had sirens going off in her head—Accident Waiting to Happen.

Oh, God. Was it a coincidence? Or was it something that came to his mind because of what was happening at the station? Or had he caused the accidents?

The investigators think that only the Dolphin accidents were sabotage, but I know the hangar accidents were too. You have to help us or someone could get killed.

Tyler's words reverberated in her brain for the second time that hour. Drew was a mechanic. He was also usually on Tyler's crew. His list proved he wasn't just pouting but seriously hated his fellow crew members, and it appeared it was escalating.

But Drew had been injured, too. She'd seen where in the hangar the accident happened and he'd started coming to her as soon as his arm had been operated on. He couldn't have done that to himself unless he was truly psychotic.

Quickly, she opened her file on Drew Linden and skimmed over her notes. No red flags popped up that would indicate a psychotic break, but now that she looked for it, she could see a pattern of anger. He was so good, she would never have found it if she wasn't looking for it.

She closed the file and collapsed on her chair. Half of her believed Drew was bent on a twisted revenge and half of her didn't believe it at all. The problem was, with what she had, she couldn't tell anyone anyway. She probably wouldn't even think it possible if Tyler hadn't put it in her head to begin with. Her objectivity had been corrupted. She would have to recommend Drew see someone else now. Crap.

You have to help us or someone could get killed.

"Oh, God." Tyler went back to his regular duty today. All the crew members were in jeopardy, whether it was Drew or someone else. Her heart squeezed at the idea that the last time she saw him she was furious. What if she was wrong? What if he did like her and just got carried away. She understood now why he might have been overzealous. Lives were at stake, even his.

She should send him a text. Maybe tell him she hoped he stayed safe.

Her office door opened and the receptionist peeked her head in. "Excuse me, Dr. Haskell, but your next appointment is here."

She clicked on her calendar and looked at the name and time. Crap, she was two minutes late. "Thank you, send him in." She rose in preparation to greet her patient. Maybe she'd text Tyler at her next break.

Tyler left the chief's office, frustrated that the chief wouldn't ground them. He understood that there was someone causing the accidents, but the surveillance tape showed nothing with all the blind spots in the hangar.

His only hope now was that the Dolphin wouldn't be needed. There were no patrols scheduled today, so if they could just get through two more hours, until after sunset, he could be sure he lived another day.

Running his hand through his hair, he strode toward his office. He couldn't trust the very people he worked with. The only Air Station person he might be able to confide in was Alix, if she was up for it. He'd like to ask Meghan if it would be okay, but she hadn't returned his call.

Walking into his office, he stopped. "What are you doing in here, Drew?"

The kid pulled out the top draw of Tyler's desk. "I'm looking for some of that pink stuff. I feel like I'm going to throw up."

"Shit kid, if you're sick, get out of here. I'll call in Steve."

Drew moved to Kolbe's desk and opened another draw. "I only have two hours. I just need some of that pink stuff."

Tyler sighed. "No, go home. That's an order. I don't want the rest of the crew getting sick."

"You're pulling rank on me?" Drew's tone made it clear he was pissed.

"Yeah, in this case I am. Go."

"Fine. If you say so." Drew gave him a mock salute and stormed out.

He wished there was a maturity test new recruits had to take because dealing with Drew was getting old. Maybe they could have the young guys work in bigger Air Stations or something so no one person would have to deal with them over an extended period of time.

Picking up the phone, he called Steve. The man wasn't happy, but he was on his way. All part of working for Uncle Sam.

A horn outside the hangar announced a delivery the chief was expecting, so Tyler headed out. As he and Kolbe carried in the equipment parts, his cell phone buzzed. He'd have to get back to that. The chief would have his head if he stopped in the middle of a delivery.

When they were finally done, they headed for the break room. Grabbing an orange juice, two granola bars and a large bag of honey roasted peanuts, he dropped into a chair across from Kolbe. He really liked the man, but he was on his suspect list, so he wouldn't relax his guard. "Do you think we'll get through today without another accident?"

Kolbe shrugged. "Don't know. Someone has cursed this place. I don't think any of us will leave this duty station unscathed."

"Really? Why would anyone want to curse us?"

Kolbe leaned forward. "You know the maritime enforcement specialist who just had a kid? The one on the Apalachee?"

"Yeah."

"I think he's in to voodoo. He's born and bred in New Orleans."

Tyler barely kept from rolling his eyes. To have the most mature person on the crews believing in curses was too crazy for him. "But why would he want to curse us?"

"I heard he wanted to be a pilot, but they failed him for being too dangerous. He wasn't too good at safety checks." Kolbe nodded like that was key.

It was interesting information, and it was plausible, but he'd only met the man once. Was Meghan right? Was he so focused on the air crews that he was missing all the other possibilities?

His phone buzzed again, so he motioned to Kolbe that he had to take it before standing and walking out of the break room. "Hey."

"Where've you been? I called you a half hour ago." Ryan's voice sounded stressed.

"Sorry, I'm on duty. What's wrong. Everything okay on the farm?"

"Yeah, we're fine, but you're not."

"What do you mean?" He strode toward his office where he could have some privacy.

"I mean, I've been doing some research on your air crew members. You're going to owe me though because I'm Army and not Coast Guard and now I have to service a Mercedes for a year."

"If there is any way it will save lives, I'm happy to owe you."

"Good. The info I got isn't classified or anything, but you'd have to put two and two together for it all to click. I was able to read up on the station reports about each member of your Air Station."

Tyler closed the door to his shared office and sat. "You really don't like construction, do you?"

"Yeah, well, this is more important. Anyway, I found a pattern of accidents followed one of your crew members. It may be a coincidence as he has only been at one other station."

"Fuck. It's Drew, isn't it?" He ran his hand through his hair as he tried to put the puzzle pieces together.

"And I think he's getting braver. The ones at the other station caused minor injuries, but always around him, so they started to call him bad luck. The last and worst injury was a broken arm."

Tyler whistled through his teeth. "You think he broke his own arm to keep suspicion off him?"

"You tell me. I also discovered that his dad worked in a factory that produced nuts and bolts. He was hurt on the job and has been on disability ever since. He ended up with a brain injury."

"Shit." He could almost feel bad for the kid. Almost.

"Where is he now?"

"I just sent him home. He said he was sick. I caught him in my office looking for that pink crap that helps settle your stomach."

"Do you believe he was sick or was he in your office to set you up? At the other station, two people were hurt twice."

"Hell, how am I going to find that out? Maybe I should just stay out of my office until something falls."

Ryan was quiet on the other end.

This sucked. He looked up at the ceiling which

was also the floor of the training room. Would it come down on him today? Tomorrow?

"Hey Tyler, where was Drew when you walked in to your office?"

He thought back. "He was in front of my desk, opening my top drawer, right beneath my computer."

"Start looking in that area for anything. This guy might even set it up for your computer to fall on your foot and break it. I'm on my way to help you look. Can you get me on base?"

He stood up and backed away from his desk. "Yeah, you're in the system. Are you at the farm?"

Ryan chuckled on the other end. "No, I'm at your house using your home computer. I used your emergency key to get in."

"My emerg—how the hell did you find that?"

"Hiding it beneath the sign that says "Coasties do it best" is not very imaginative. I'm heading out now."

"Don't forget to lock the fucking door."

Ryan laughed as he hung up.

Tyler ran his hand through his hair and stared at his desk. What could the kid have done? First, he needed to get Ryan on base. Still standing, he grabbed the wireless keyboard and put it on a bookcase. As soon as he hit a key, the screen saver went off on his computer and his email list appeared.

He hadn't checked his email since lunchtime. Why was it the open screen? He took a couple steps closer to his computer to look at the last message that came in. Nothing had changed. Glancing at his sent messages, he stopped. There was an unknown email address in there.

He clicked to view the sent message. "Fucking-A."

HI MEGHAN, I'D LIKE TO TAKE YOU TO ROCK ISLAND TO WATCH THE SUNSET. MEET ME AT THE YARDARM DOCKS AT 16:30. SEE YOU THEN.

He felt like a rogue wave had just taken him down. He glanced at his watch. Fuck! It was 17:00. Pulling out his phone he dialed Ryan.

"Hello?"

"The fucker took Meghan! Do me a favor and go straight to Yardarm docks and see if they left yet. He told her to meet him there at 16:30. Shit, if he does anything to her, I'm going to kill him."

"Got it. On my way. Call the police and tell them you think you there's been an abduction. But first call Meghan and see if she went. You said she was mad at you, so maybe she ignored the message or didn't get it."

"Right." Tyler hung up the phone and immediately dialed Meghan.

⌒

Meghan thanked the cashier at the dock store for the ice tea and walked outside. The weather was perfect for a boat ride. She'd even worn shorts and a t-shirt for the occasion.

She strolled to the picnic bench near the river and sat. She was early as usual. She almost didn't come. Tyler didn't ask. He just assumed she'd be here. Then again, maybe he was just hoping she would be. In turn, she hadn't responded. As she had said, what was good for the goose was good for the gander.

If she hadn't met with Drew, she probably wouldn't have come at all, but the need to make sure Tyler wasn't hurt was too much. She thought he got off shift at six, but maybe he had someone cover for him. She couldn't deny the gesture.

She'd looked up Rock Island and it was a long way out, the last island before the Gulf and only accessible by boat. The view would be even more spectacular than at his house. She had yet to go out on any of the rivers and into the Gulf so that did entice her. She hoped it was calm.

She really didn't believe Drew would cause his crewmates harm. If he really was that angry at them, she was fairly sure he'd want to be there when they were hurt because it would be very personal. But except for Tyler's accident, Drew hadn't been around. At least not from what he'd told her. Besides, he was hurt as well. It had to be an outside person.

"Dr. Haskell?"

Startled from her thoughts, she turned. "Drew? What are you doing here?"

He gave her a sheepish grin. "Tyler asked me to help him out. He wants me to bring you out to Rock Island. I think he's setting up a surprise for you."

She pasted on a smile. "But I thought you weren't happy about me seeing Tyler."

"I wasn't because I thought you'd talk about me. I didn't realize you can't say anything. After I went to work, I searched on the internet. It says that you'll go to jail if you divulge anything about our sessions, sort of like lawyer-client confidentiality. I know all about that. So, I'm fine with you dating Tyler."

Relief washed through her. Her confidentiality rules were a little different from a lawyer's, but if it made him feel better, then she was fine with it. "I have a question for you. Do you like Tyler?"

Drew shrugged. "Sure. Why?"

She couldn't discuss his session in a public place like they were in, so she refrained, but there was more than one way to figure out if he really was okay with Tyler. "I guess it would make me feel better if I knew you liked him. I don't know him that well. You've known him a lot longer than I have."

He appeared to give the question serious consideration. "I guess if you're going to date someone at the station, Tyler's not a bad choice."

Hmm, that wasn't quite as revealing as she had

hoped. "Well, before we go, I want to let Tyler know I'm here. I didn't have time to reply to his email." She pulled out her cell phone.

"That won't work."

She stilled. "Why?"

He gave her an apologetic smile. "There's no cell service out by Rock Island. That's why we rely on the radios when we are out that far."

Oh, that made sense. "Okay, then I guess we better get going."

Drew was the perfect gentleman as he helped her into the twenty-foot fiberglass boat with the word Bayliner down its side. It had a driver console at the front on the starboard side. There was seating directly behind that, but for conversation's sake, she sat of the port side, across from Drew.

As they moved away from the docks and through the waterways, he was careful. As he explained, it was very shallow. "We'll be able to go faster once we get out into the Gulf."

She frowned. "But I thought the island is *before* the Gulf."

"Oh, it is, but you can't get to it from the river side because it's swampy. The only approach is from the Gulf, but it has a really nice sandy beach. I bet Tyler will get a fire going."

At the thought of her and Tyler on a secluded island, she started to get excited. It didn't appear as if Drew was a threat, and now she felt bad for having her doubts.

As they meandered down the river, she pulled out her phone and texted Tyler. At least when he saw her, she could say she'd responded. She told him she was on her way with Drew.

"What are you doing?" Drew scowled.

"I was just texting Tyler so when we get back in, he will see I did respond."

"Stupid." Drew slapped her hand and her phone flew out of the boat.

"What are you doing? That's my work phone."

He put the boat in neutral and grabbed both her hands. "I'm sorry Dr. Haskell, but Tyler doesn't deserve you."

CHAPTER TEN

Meghan pulled away, falling half over the side as she did so.

"Oh no, not yet." Drew grabbed one of her hands, and she reached her other into her purse for her pepper spray, but before she could get it, he kicked her legs out from under her and she fell to the deck.

Oh, God. She'd never been one for a lot of physical activity, but she kicked and scratched as well as she could, until he rolled her over onto her stomach.

She stared at the life jackets under the seats on the starboard side of the boat, wishing now that she had donned one. Whatever he planned for her, wasn't going to end well.

Once he tied her hands behind her back, he pulled her up on to the portside seat. "Now stay there." He turned his back on her and redirected the boat which had floated into a marshy area, no doubt filled with alligators.

She needed to do something. Maybe if she jumped out while they were going slower and still in shallow waters, she'd have a chance. She looked at the shoreline to see three alligators basking in the sun.

She swallowed. There were no roads out this far but maybe there would be a cottage or something on one of the many islands made from the rivers. If she could get people to notice her, she could yell for them to call the police. "Why are you doing this? I've never hurt you. I've been trying to help you."

Drew shook his head. "Only because the government made you. I know how the system works. Screw the little guy." He laughed. "But sometimes the little guy gets his revenge."

He expertly maneuvered the boat between two islands, the narrow passageway was shallow. There were no alligators in sight, so she leaned to look over the side. Two eyes met her gaze. Crap! That plan was obviously not going to work. "Do you mean you're the one that has caused all the accidents at the Air Station?" She needed to keep him distracted.

He smiled. "You bet. They were ingenious. Just accidents."

"But you got hurt, too."

He refocused on his driving, steering the boat away from rocks. "Yeah, that was supposed to be Kolbe. I set it up for him to help me, but then he went to the bathroom. I thought I had enough time to grab the tool and get away, but the freaking thing came down on me." He looked back at her. "Turned out that was a benefit. Who would ever suspect me?"

There was a cut out in the fiberglass of the boat which allowed for additional storage next to the seat she was on, so she turned half way and put the rope against the sharp edge and started to saw while watching Drew's every movement. It looked a hell of a lot easier in the movies. She had to stop after a minute because her arms ached.

"Was Tyler's accident planned as well?"

Drew chuckled. "That was my masterpiece. All I had to do is stash the ratcheting cable cutter in the Dolphin when no one was around. Then I simply cut the cable and dropped the cutter into the sea after it. No one was the wiser."

Drew paused as he started to increase their speed. "My only misplay on that one was that I thought we were over more shallow water, but it was dark, and we moved quite a bit to pull Tyler out after the victim was in the helo."

He turned and looked at her. "Just think, if Tyler had died that night, you wouldn't be here right now. Isn't that a strange thought?"

She stared in shock. How could she have missed the signs? The man was a genius at hiding this side of him. She went back to sawing on the ropes, but it didn't feel like she was making progress. She hoped he planned to drop her on Rock Island and leave her there, then she might have a chance.

But what if he just dropped her in the middle of the Gulf?

As they came around a bend in the river, the Gulf in all its yellow and orange glory came into view and Drew threw the throttle down causing her to fall from the seat on to the deck. "Ack."

He looked behind him and laughed, but didn't help her. Squirming her way over to the starboard side, she righted herself. The Gulf looked beautiful, but menacing as the waves grew higher and they bounced along.

It was no use talking now. He wouldn't hear her over the wind. One of the life vests under the seat fell forward when they hit a particularly high wave. Turning so her back was against the seat as she sat on the deck, she reached her tied hands back as far as she could and grasped the life vest.

As she watched Drew, she pulled the strap around her bound hands. The clip had to be there somewhere. Another large bump sent her sliding away from the seat and jarred her teeth. She started to tear up, her frustration and fear getting the better of her.

God Tyler. I'm so sorry I didn't forgive you. You were right.

At the thought of Tyler, she couldn't help going over all his wonderful traits in her mind. It was a comfort even if it was useless. He had a big heart. He always played it safe. He was strong enough emotionally not to need counseling after his fall from the helicopter.

He was strong enough? Yes, he would never give up in a situation like this. Gathering her strength, she scooted back to the seat and wrapped the life jacked cord around her tied hands again. She braced her feet against the bumps to keep herself in place, taking the brunt of the jarring against her back as it hit the seat.

Finally, she felt the clip snap into place. She had one life vest attached, though in an awkward spot, but it had to be better than nothing. If her ropes let go, the life vest would no longer be attached, but then her hands would be free to put it on.

Drew slowed the boat and in a panic, she flicked her sandals off and pulled another life vest around her ankle with her foot. Then she crouched and got her butt up on the starboard seat, the life vest she attached wedged firmly between her and the seat.

Drew appeared to be looking for a particular spot. His slicked-back blonde hair now a mess from the wind and looking purple in the dying light.

Oh God, she would be out here in the dark. She looked back the way they had come. She could just make out the mouth of the river. Following Drew's gaze, she could see a large marshy area that bled into the Gulf.

The waves buffeted the boat, making it rock precariously. The motion caused her stomach to roll over in discomfort.

"There it is!" Drew pointed, his excitement obvious.

She peered into the Eastern darkness and barely made out a small island in the middle of the marshy mess. He turned and looked at her. "That's Rock Island. I'm delivering you as promised. I'm afraid I can't get any closer, so you'll have to get off here."

He didn't even sound sarcastic as if he really felt like he was fulfilling an obligation.

She just had to ask. "Is Tyler there?"

He laughed. "For a smart woman, you can be so dumb. Tyler doesn't know about your little assignation. I'm the one who sent the email to you from his computer. Stupid guy doesn't even know he sent it. And I'm home in bed because I'm sick."

Suddenly, the reality of her next twenty-four hours, if she could make it that long, loomed up in scary terror. She had to try something. "Can't you leave me on another island? What if Tyler does find his email. He might come looking for me."

"No." Drew's answer was immediate. "This is how I planned it. We do it this way." He stepped in front of her. "Time for you to get off." As he grabbed her, his foot caught on the life vest that was hooked around her ankle.

"What's this?" He pulled it from her foot and laughed. "You want a life jacket? Here you go." He flung the jacket over the side.

"Please, Drew. Don't do this."

"Please Drew, don't do this." He repeated her plea in a falsetto voice. Then he sneered. "I'm done with you."

Before she realized what he planned to do, he'd pulled her up against him and pushed her over the side.

⁓

Tyler left a message on Meghan's voice mail, but his gut told him she wasn't going to get it. He had to call the police.

A text message ding came in on his phone. Like he had time for that. Clicking on it quickly, he froze. It was sent thirty minutes ago. The bastard had her.

He dialed the police and explained the situation. They said they'd send a boat out immediately and told him to contact the Coast Guard. Really?

He dialed Ryan as he walked to the Chief's office. "I got a text from her. Drew has her."

"Damn. Did you call the police?"

"Yeah, they're taking a boat out but they said to call the Coast Guard."

"What are you going to do?"

"I'm going to find her." He hung up and walked into the Chief's office.

He was out of there in less than five minutes, the Chief's curses following him out the door. "Kolbe, Sam, Steve, we have a SAR!" He immediately suited up in his swim gear while his fellow crew members followed their routines.

Within minutes he was in the Dolphin and Sam had the rotors going. He just hoped that Drew hadn't done anything to the helo. The call came in as they lifted off and the Search and Rescue became official. *Thanks Chief.*

He had himself wedged against the water pump and kept his eyes on the floor. Even so, he knew how high they were flying and his breathing turned shallow. He had to do this. He *had* to save Meghan.

He closed his eyes and reviewed memories of her. Her calm air, her intelligence, her amazing colored eyes when she took off her glasses.

"Hey, Tyler. You okay?"

He opened his eyes to see Steve frowning at him. Behind him it was pitch black outside the windows. That seemed to help. He nodded. "Yeah. Just praying. Dr. Haskell and I are in a relationship."

Steve's wide eyes made it clear he hadn't known. "Do Sam and Kolbe know?"

He shook his head. "Want me to tell them?"

"Yes." He wanted everyone to know. She was one of them. Kolbe turned around and spoke into his headset. "You have good taste, man. We'll find her."

He gave him a thumbs up, but stayed where he was. Did the bastard leave her stranded on that island? He didn't even know which one it was. Half the little islands along the delta had no names. Sam had the coordinates. She would find the island, but would they find Meghan? Or Meghan's body?

All of them were issued a Sig Sauer. Would Drew shoot Meghan and leave her body on the island? The sudden thought had his heart pounding so hard he grabbed his chest.

Fuck, he loved her.

—

Instinctually, Meghan held her breath as the warm water of the Gulf in summer surrounded her. She kicked upward and took in air as her head broke the surface. Though she had the life preserver clipped to her hands, she still grasped it for the life line it was.

Drew waited for her to come up then revved the engines and spun the boat around, adding to the waves and throwing water over her. She coughed as she continued to kick to keep her head above the water with no hands.

The life jacket tried to push her forward, so she maneuvered it beneath her butt. That helped, but she still needed to use her feet to stay upright. There was very little light in the sky, just a tiny sheen still left bouncing across the waves. It wasn't much, but it did show her the other life jacket floating away.

Her eyes filled with tears. She should have listened to Tyler. She wouldn't be out in the Gulf with her hands tied behind her back if she had. Did he know she was out here or did he head home from work, thinking that she was still mad at him?

None of that would help her now. It was time to take some of her own advice. It was easy to tell Alix that she could still have a life, but now Meghan had to prove that she could handle a traumatic event herself. Looking around, she could just make out the blurry lights of a boat heading the opposite way of the horizon. Her glasses had come off as she fell into the Gulf, so it wasn't very clear. She needed to move in the direction of that boat before she drifted too far into the Gulf.

But too close to shore and she'd have to contend with alligators. What would Tyler do? He always played it safe. What was safe? Keeping land in sight. She might get lucky and a boat heading into the river might see her.

With no other option, she kicked herself in the general direction of where she thought the river was. When a large wave hit her, she stopped kicking to save her energy. Though the water was warm this time of year, it definitely wasn't body temperature. She could see herself dying of hypothermia before ever getting picked up.

Okay, if I get close to land, I will brave the alligators to get out of the water. Having a plan made her feel productive, so she continued her never-ending trek towards the river. Kicking forward, resting with the waves. She refused to give up even though she couldn't see a single light anywhere.

The flight to the coast felt longer than usual. He wanted to be there. To find Meghan. It didn't help that he was sweating profusely, but at least his stomach had stopped trying to come up.

Kolbe turned around and spoke into the head set. "We just got word the police caught Drew on his way in."

"Is Meghan with him?"

Kolbe turned back to talk to Sector.

Tyler felt like ever part of his body was wound as tight as an anchor winch. If he heard good news, he'd probably fall just as fast.

Kolbe spoke again. "That's negative. Drew is claiming that he has no idea what they are talking about."

"Fuck. Did he have his Sig with him?" Once again, he had to wait.

Finally, Kolbe answered. "Negative."

Relief washed through Tyler at the news. "That means we have to find her. How close are we to this Rock Island?"

"ETA is two minutes."

Tyler focused on adjusting his equipment and getting ready. If she was in the water or on the island, he would find her. If she had a life jacket on, they just needed to worry about hypothermia. If she was unconscious on an island, they had to worry about animals. If she was unconscious and in the water without a life jacket, then she…

He couldn't even go there. She was alive. He had to believe that.

"Turning on the search light." Sam's voice came over the headsets.

In other words, they all needed to look out the windows for Meghan. He swallowed hard. He *would* do this.

Forcing himself to the side, he looked down to the inky black water as his stomach crawled up his throat. Darkness started to crowd his vision and he closed his eyes against it. He would not pass out. Meghan needed him.

Opening his eyes again, he forced himself to look.

The Dolphin circled the island first, very low, but there was no evidence of anyone there. No footprints and no drag marks. That meant Meghan was in the water.

He swallowed as Sam made a wider loop to view the swampy area around the small piece of land. Still no sign of her. God, he hoped she hadn't been in that mess.

Sam then started the usual search pattern which put them higher.

Again, he felt himself losing vision and he closed his eyes against it, even as he swallowed the bile that came up into his mouth. Snapping his eyes open again he studied the waves.

"There!" He yelled over the headset. "Four o'clock."

Sam circled around, but flew lower. There was definitely something there. But if it was a person, they weren't waving or anything. Was it Meghan and was she conscious? He looked at his watch. She could have been in the water for over an hour already. "Lower."

He took off his head set and donned his fins and adjusted his mask, refusing to think about the fact he would have to go down. He moved toward the edge, but didn't look over.

Steve grinned. "At least you don't have to worry about Drew. No more accidents."

Holy shit! Steve was right. In his worry for Meghan, he'd forgotten that. No cut cable this time. He swung his legs over the side and gave Steve the thumbs up. Then he jumped.

The water went over him and he popped back up. Now he was in his element. He couldn't see anything nearby in the ink darkness so he looked up at Steve who pointed.

Tyler set out, keeping his strokes even until he crested a wave and saw the object they'd found. It was definitely Meghan, but she wasn't facing him. There was no way she would hear him over the Dolphin's blades, so he didn't call out, but swam faster. When he reached her, he spun her around. "Meghan!"

She looked at him in shock, but didn't hang on to him. Everyone who was rescued tried to hang on. "Meghan, are you okay?"

She shook her head even as her teeth chattered. "Tied…tied…my…hands."

His heart went into double time as he reached around her with one arm and found her hands tied together behind her back. He held her to him as he used his other hand to pull his knife out and saw at the water-logged rope.

He couldn't keep them afloat and get through the rope.

He signaled for the basket. "We're going to get you into the helo. Then I'll get that rope off you."

She didn't respond, her teeth chattering the only movement in her face. When the basket dropped, he tilted it and pulled her torso onto it first. Then he brought her legs up and gave the thumbs up.

As he watched the woman he loved be pulled into the Dolphin, his whole body seemed to uncoil with relief. Usually, at this point in a rescue, he enjoyed the moment while he waited for the cable, floating with the sea enjoying his success, but tonight he was impatient.

When the cable finally came down, he grabbed on and started to rise, a vision of himself falling flashed through his mind and he pushed it away. Drew was gone and he wanted to be with Meghan, no matter how high he was.

As he entered the helo, Steve slammed the door shut and Sam headed for land. Tyler whipped off his helmet and fins and pulled his knife from his vest again.

Steve had Meghan covered in blankets. He looked at her but her eyes were closed and her breaths shallow. "Come on Meghan, stay with me." Gently, he rolled her to her side, motioning Steve to hold her there. It took him a good five minutes to get everything cut off including the life jacket. He was glad he hadn't tried any longer in the ocean.

How she managed to hook a life jacket was beyond him, but he was thankful she had. Even he would have a hard time staying afloat with his hands tied behind his back.

Rage at Drew started deep in his belly, but he squashed it. Meghan was his priority. He rubbed her wrists to get the blood flowing again, her hands already showing tinges of blue. Then he rolled her back over and tucked the blankets around her. He knelt next the basket and brushed her wet hair from her face. "Meghan?"

She didn't respond.

He needed her to remain conscious, so he kissed her. At first her salty lips remained still, but as he put his soul into the kiss, she moaned. When she started to kiss him back, he wanted to laugh with relief.

He broke the kiss and whispered against her lips. "I love you."

CHAPTER ELEVEN

Meghan sipped her chardonnay as she sat on the patio at Tyler's house. He'd gone back in for cheese and crackers. She really didn't need food. What she needed was him.

She took another sip, mainly to calm her nerves, as the sunlight off the Gulf sparkled like glitter. Over the last three days, Tyler had been amazing. Calling her sister, who came right away while she was still in the hospital, telling her receptionist to reschedule her appointments until next week, even taking leave so he could cook for her.

His words in the helicopter had seemed almost too good to be true. She knew dangerous, adrenaline-spiking situations could give people a false sense of closeness, which is why she hadn't mentioned what he said. At the time, his words had warmed her heart, keeping her alert. His kisses hadn't hurt either.

That's why she hadn't been sure if she should believe him. Her mother always said that actions spoke louder than words. After the last three days, she was completely sure he still felt as he had in the helicopter.

Her nerves were more because she expected that he would want to make love tonight. He hadn't said it. Hadn't even hinted at it, but her instinct was screaming at her that it was the probable ending to their day.

She took another swallow of wine. She was nervous because before they did that, she needed to tell him how she felt. After her hour in the sea to think about her life and everything she hadn't done, she had a new perspective.

The sliding glass door opened and Tyler strode out. She sucked in her breath. He'd taken off his shirt and wore only a pair of shorts, not even flip flops. He had swimmer muscles times two—broad shoulders, mounded pectoral muscles and ripped abs that looked harder than a turtle shell. His large biceps tapered to his elbow but then his forearms boasted their own muscle. His entire torso was spattered with light freckles and she suddenly had the urge to lick every one.

"Here you go. Hope you don't mind extra sharp cheese." He placed the plate on an end table set in front of their two chairs.

She moved her glasses to the top of her head as he came close and swallowed to get her throat to work again. "That's fine." She clamped her mouth shut before she could tell him she felt over dressed in her pale-yellow sundress and white heels.

He pulled his iron chair with the soft pad on it against hers and sat.

At that she couldn't help but smile. "If you got any closer you'd be in my lap." She winked.

Tyler grinned. "Excellent idea."

Before she could take another breath, he'd lifted her from her own chair and settled her on his lap.

"Ack." Some of the wine spilled on her wrist with his move.

"Here, I'll take care of that." He gently turned her wrist to face him, brought it to his mouth and licked.

A shiver of excitement raced across her skin.

When he finished licking far more than where the wine was, he lifted his head to look at her. "Better?"

She nodded, unable to form words while her blood was overheating.

"Good. Now we are set to watch the sunset." He glanced away to examine the horizon. Then as if he'd calculated the exact time the best colors would show, he picked up a cracker with cheese and held it to her mouth. "Hungry?"

She was, but more for him than the cheese. Still, obediently she opened her mouth and as he slid the cracker and cheese into her mouth, she bit it in half and chewed.

His gaze never left her lips.

Crap, the man was beyond intoxicating. Who needed wine with him around? When she finished with that piece, she opened her lips and he slid the second half of the cracker into her mouth. She closed her lips on his finger and thumb and licked.

His eyes darkened and his nostrils flared. "Meghan."

Her heart skipped a beat as he gazed at her, and she almost forgot to chew. As soon as she swallowed, she answered him. "Tyler."

His lip quirked up on the side.

"I never thanked you for saving me. I never expected to be in such a situation and then all you've done for me these past three days, well, you've gone above and beyond."

He frowned. "Not even close. I was the one who put you in danger. I can never make that up to you."

"I think I did that all by myself. I should have known you wouldn't send me an email like that. I was too anxious to see you, make sure you were safe. I wasn't thinking straight."

The hand he had resting on her back moved up and grasped her neck. "If I had lost you…." He pulled her to him and kissed her, his tongue breaching her lips immediately and sweeping inside as if reassuring himself she was still with him.

She'd never felt so wanted…so loved. She held on to him with one arm, reassuring him she was still alive. Maybe even reassuring herself as tingles of desire threaded their way from her breasts to her groin.

He broke the kiss to pull back just far enough to look at her.

It was now or never. She gazed into his dark gray eyes. "I love you."

He smiled, his face brighter than any sunset. "Thank God, because I could never let you go."

She returned his smile as warmth spread from her heart to the ends of her finger tips. She wanted to hug him, but she still held her wine glass in one hand. Maybe he sensed her need because he pulled her closer, hugging her with steely strength, but gently as if she were precious. Her heart soared higher than any helicopter.

When he relaxed, allowing them to look at each other again, she felt the need to reassure him. "Don't worry. I'm not going anywhere, especially not back in the ocean. In fact, I'm not going swimming ever again unless it's in a pool." She'd meant her statement to be funny, but his brow lowered and his gray eyes grew lighter with intensity.

"You need to face your fear. Trust me, I know. It's the only way to overcome it and get your life back."

Her life back? Wait, he wasn't talking about her. "What do you know about fear? You fell from a helicopter, broke both legs and went right back on board."

He looked at the sunset, and she glanced that way to see if that truly held his attention, but the colors were muted by gathering clouds.

"Tyler?"

He finally returned his gaze to her. "Fear is what kept me from asking you out sooner. I was afraid that since you were a psychologist, you'd discover my fear. After the accident, I developed a fear of heights."

She pulled back. "You did?"

He nodded. "Remember the escalator ride in the mall?"

She thought back to that. He'd said he didn't feel well because of a muscle cramp in his back. A plausible explanation, but all his symptoms, shortness of breath, perspiration, everything, were typical of acrophobia. She should have known if she wasn't so distracted by him. "Why didn't you tell me or come see me."

He looked away again. "I didn't want to admit it. I've never had an issue with heights. My job is to jump from helos. How could I admit I was afraid of heights to anyone? But I knew I needed help because I would have to go up in a bird eventually when I returned to regular duty. I decided to see Dr. Preston."

"So you weren't seeing him for anger management issues then?"

"Anger man—no. I have no problem with my anger. I just needed to kick the fear to the curb."

She stroked his back with her hand, loving the feel of his warm skin. "I guess he was able to help because you came to get me." She smiled, pleased that he got the help he needed.

He shook his head, and she stilled her hand. "Actually, it was you who got me back in the Dolphin. Dr. Preston gave me a plan of action, to discover why I fell. That helped me stay sane. But it was your danger that had me crawling back into that helo, even though I was about to vomit all over it."

"Oh my, God. You went up there with that fear? You are even braver than I gave you credit for. I've counselled a couple phobias and they are truly debilitating."

He gave her a weak smile. "I know it was wrong and my chief would have my head if he knew, but I'm glad I never went to see you for professional help. I much prefer a more personal approach." He wiggled his brows to punctuate his statement.

He was right. She wouldn't be sitting on his lap right now if he'd come to her like he was supposed to. She never would have believed he'd circumvent the rules, but he had and she was grateful. So grateful, she had to kiss him again.

He kissed her right back, making her feel loved and sexy at the same time. Then he broke the kiss and she pouted. She could sit there all night kissing him.

"Look." He turned his head to look out at the Gulf.

She meant to glance at the sunset, but found herself enthralled by it. The sun had dipped below the clouds to touch the water, squeezing out a spectacular array of colors from bright orange to pink to red to purple. "That's amazing."

Tyler's husky voice in her ear caught her off guard. "You're amazing." His words and breath sent a shiver down her spine that ignited all her passion zones. She wrapped her arms around his neck, wine glass and all, and tipped her head to the side as he kissed his way from her ear to her collar bone.

He lifted his arm, pushing hers upward and causing her wine to spill down the front of her dress. She started, but Tyler didn't let her go far. He just gazed at her wet dress showing her chemise beneath and the outline of her nipple.

Then his gaze met hers. "I have found a new appreciation for wine. Don't drop the glass too, or it will shatter on the concrete." He lowered his face and began to lick his way from her collar bone to her cleavage, following the wet liquid.

She still held the glass in one hand and her other arm was pinned between him and the chair, she had no choice but to let him do as he would. And she had no complaints.

With his teeth, he pulled her cotton neckline below her wet breast and laved the silky chemise over her hard nub. When his teeth latched on to it, she squirmed, wanting to grasp his head to her, but unable to because of the wine glass.

With his hand, he pulled the chemise up from

under her dress and bunched it against her neck then blew on her nipple. He glanced up at her for a second before he lowered his head and licked. Tingles started there and went straight to her core.

Tyler's licks soon became nibbles and her sheath moistened. When he suddenly sucked, she moaned and one of her legs fell off his lap, her foot finding purchase on the patio. His sucking grew harder then softer and harder again, and she pressed her hips upward in response, unable to keep still as her desire built.

When he left her breast, she gasped in much needed air, her breaths having shortened so much she was slightly light headed. As her hips came down, she felt the hard ridge of his erection against her butt.

He moved his talented mouth over her dress to her other breast, which no longer had a chemise protecting it. He sucked the tip, dress and all, into his mouth. When he bit at her nipple, she moaned louder, her foot on the patio now stabilizing her ability to push her hips toward him.

She closed her eyes, unable to focus on anything but the feelings coursing through her.

Tyler's hand released her chemise, though his mouth did not release her nipple. She wanted to call him back, but before she could, his hand was on her knee and moving her dress upward.

Oh, yes. She moved her leg aside more, allowing

him free access to her silk panties. While he feasted on her breast through the dress, his other hand moved between her legs and stroked upward over her opening and clit.

He tugged on her nipple before looking up at her. "You're wet."

Panting, she forced a swallow. "You made me that way."

His grin was downright exhilarating. "I like wet."

He returned his mouth to her over sensitized nipples, but his fingers were burrowing beneath her panties to play. He explored her as she arched against his arm, anxious to feel him touch her. Instead, he played with each fold, slightly skimming her opening then brushing against her clit to stroke her small patch of hair.

She wanted completion, but he kept her near the edge, promising, teasing, but not delivering. Desperate, she opened her eyes and lowered her hips, rubbing her butt against his cock. The nylon shorts didn't hide anything, and she heard his quick intake of breath.

Finally, his fingers moved back to her sheath and he pushed one inside her.

"Ahhh."

At her sound, he looked at her, her nipple between his teeth and he watched her as he sawed back and forth across her nub.

She bucked, and he withdrew his finger only to add another and slide them inside.

He sucked her nipple hard, sending pleasure washing over her like a wave. His fingers started to pump in and out.

She closed her eyes again and lifted her hips, anxious for where he was taking her.

Then he pulled his fingers out and focused on her clit, circling it, rubbing it, stroking it. He played her body like a master and just as she peaked, he slid his fingers inside her and pumped hard, making her body reverberate with pleasure. He grasped her head and gave her a mind shattering kiss.

When she finally opened her eyes, he pulled his mouth away, allowing her to take the deep breaths she needed.

"You're so beautiful when you come."

She couldn't respond to that if she tried, but it definitely made her cheeks warm.

He slowly slid his fingers from between her legs and licked them. "You taste perfect. I want to eat you, but I can't wait to be inside you."

Just as her heartbeat was slowing, his words picked it back up. She nodded, not sure if she could stand quite yet, but anxious to have him inside her and give him equal pleasure.

He must have taken the wine glass from her because she no longer had it in her hand and she spied it on the table that he pushed out of the way with his foot. Beneath her butt, she could feel exactly how much he wanted her and her body revved in anticipation.

She moved her other foot to the patio and Tyler helped her stand. She took a step and her knees wobbled. "I don't think I'll make it to your bedroom."

"Who needs a bedroom." He walked her the four steps around the wicker couch.

Somewhere in the back of her mind, she understood that she was outside making love where anyone on the water might see them in the light from the house that shone on the patio, but she was too excited to care.

She leaned her butt against the back of it as he stripped off his shorts. She grabbed the couch to keep standing. Tyler was thick, long and ready for her. Her breaths suddenly grew short again. He stepped up to her and pulled her dress over her head.

She must look a wreck. Her hair had come out of her ponytail, her chemise was still stuck under one breast and her panties were half off. But when she looked in Tyler's eyes, she saw only desire and love.

He knelt at her feet and took off her panties, carefully getting them around her wedge sandals. Then he lifted her chemise from her. "How did I get so lucky?" His admiration added to her pleasure.

"I was just thinking the same thing."

He pulled her against him, his cock pressed

between them as her breasts crushed against his chest. He whispered in her ear. "I can't ever lose you."

She hugged him to her, titillated and happier than she'd ever been.

He pulled back. "I can't wait."

His words sent more wetness to gather in her folds. She nodded mutely.

He turned her, wrapping his arms around her before sliding his hands up her tummy to cup her breasts. His thumbs brushed her already alert nipples. "Bend over."

Tyler had wanted to make love to Meghan in his bedroom with candles and wine and flowers, but he couldn't wait. He smirked, at least they had the wine.

As she bent over the back of the wicker couch, he didn't release her breasts, loving how full they were. Her nipples were so responsive, he could spend a whole day paying homage to them. But not now.

He squeezed her breasts, before releasing them to run his hands along her sides to her perfect ass. She was *his*. What he'd wanted for months.

She braced her hands on the couch and at his touch to her ass, arched her back, giving him a glimpse of the pussy between her legs.

That was another area he planned to explore later. He squeezed her cheeks then moved his hands to the inside of her thighs, nudging her legs apart further. He couldn't resist running his fingers over her wet folds to stroke her clit.

When she shuddered, his own control slipped. He couldn't stay away from her wet sheath any longer. Quickly, he grabbed his shorts and pulled the condom out that he'd slipped in earlier, just in case. In record time, he rolled it on his cock.

Meghan laughed. "I like a man that plays it safe."

He grinned then took his cock in his hand and slid it along the wetness of her folds. He held her hip with one hand as he guided his tip to her opening. Letting his cock go, he grasped both her hips and slowly pushed inside.

Shit, she was tight and hot. His balls tightened but he held back until he was completed sheathed.

She looked behind her, and he gritted his teeth. "Don't move."

Her sly smile warned him a second before she squeezed his cock within her.

"Fuck." As he pulled his hips back and held hers still, he wasn't sure past the rushing sound in his ears, but he thought he heard her giggle just before her sudden intake of breath. He thrust forward until his pelvis smacked her ass and she moaned with pleasure.

More than happy to oblige, he pulled out and pumped into her again and again. Her moans turned to little shouts as he pistoned into the hotness that was the woman he loved. The wicker couch started to slide forward, as if she were escaping him.

He was having none of that. He grasped Meghan by her shoulder with one hand to hold her with him and thrust harder, faster.

Her scream of ecstasy sent his control out the window and he came. Satisfaction, simple and sweet suffused his soul. Her tight sheath squeezed the last drop from him, and he bent over her to hug her tight. He kissed the shell of her ear. "I love you."

Her contented sigh was all he needed to hear.

EPILOGUE

Meghan glanced up at the sign that hung over the dirt driveway then looked at Tyler. "Why do they call this place Broken Oak? That's a strange name for a horse farm."

"Wait, you'll see."

Happy to be checking out the place she'd been invited to work at, she patiently waited. She hadn't committed to the position yet, but with both Jessie and Tyler singing its praises, she had agreed to take a look.

As Tyler drove around a grove of trees, the reason for the name became clear. "That's an amazing tree."

He smiled. "And the people who live here and who will live here are amazing as well."

Ah, now she understood. They could all grow, live and even love beyond horrific events like the split oak tree that was the farm's namesake. She liked the metaphor.

Tyler pulled up in front of a freshly painted two-story home with a wide porch along the front. He jumped out of his truck and opened her door. "Did I mention how hot you look in a pair of jeans and sneakers?"

She laughed, happier inside than she ever remembered being. "Yes, you did. Twice already."

He winked at her as she pulled down the simple tan blazer she wore over her white tank. Tyler seemed to enjoy her attempts at more casual clothing, or rather enjoyed getting her out of it.

The screen door on the porch slammed and a woman about her age jogged down the steps. She really looked like a cowgirl with her straw cowboy hat, short sleeved buttoned down white shirt, jean shorts and cowboy boots.

She ran up to Tyler and gave him a hug. "Good to see you again, Tyler." Letting him go, she turned toward Meghan. "You must be the Doc. Hi, my name is Lynzie."

Lynzie's southern accent was so charming, Meghan was able to forgive her for hugging Tyler. She held out her hand. "I'm Dr. Meghan Haskell."

Lynzie ignored her hand. "Oh, we give hugs around here." Then she wrapped her arms around her.

She liked Lynzie already and smiled her approval over her shoulder at Tyler who looked very pleased with himself.

"Hey sis, don't I get a hug too?"

She spun around at the sound of Jessie's voice and

smiled with tears in her eyes. Jessie looked amazing as she strode toward her, the hitch in her step ignored. She wasn't nearly as lean as she had been and her face was tan from being in the sun, which made her look healthy and showed off her dark hair. Farm life must agree with her.

Meghan opened her arms and hugged her sister hard. She hadn't seen her in almost a year after all. Jessie even smelled good, like hay, wood and outdoors.

Jessie pretended to struggle. "Have you been lifting weights? I swear you're hugging the breath from me."

She laughed and let her sister go. "You look fantastic."

"Right, especially with sawdust all over my jeans." She looked behind her. "Cooper, come here and meet my sister."

The man walked forward slowly but purposefully. He had to be at least six foot six and his shoulders were so wide she wondered if he could fit through doorways. His buzz cut was a little long like it'd been done a month ago, and his brown hair might be wavy if let to grow.

"Okay Tank, I'd like you to meet Dr. Meghan Haskell."

The pride in Jessie's voice surprised Meghan and she reached out her hand. "It's a pleasure to meet you Cooper."

"Ma'am, the pleasure is mine." He gave her a soft smile and she immediately liked him.

Lynzie practically bounced toward the steps. "Okay, come on in everyone. We made us a big lunch."

Cooper stepped next to her and lowered his head to speak. "Lynzie's idea of big isn't the same as mine."

Meghan laughed and hooked Tyler's arm as they all moseyed inside. The lunch was sandwiches and while most of them had one or two, Cooper had seven at her last count. Tyler even stopped at four.

Ryan clinked his glass with a fork. "We all know why Dr. Haskell really came to visit us today."

Jessie grinned. "Of course, to see me." They all chuckled, but Meghan loved that her sister appeared to be in a much happier state than last time she'd seen her.

Lynzie shook her head. "Of course not. She already knows you. She came to see who could possibly have married such a crazy man as my husband."

"Gee thanks, Lynz." Ryan pretended to be hurt before his lip quirked up.

Tyler squeezed her hand beneath the table and she looked at him. He didn't say a word, but his eyes glowed with love.

"No, we are here to see if we can convince Dr. Haskell, Meghan, to come work here."

Everyone at the table smiled except Cooper. She focused on him. "Cooper, are you unsure about this?"

He shook his head. "No, just not excited about having to build another house."

"House?" She looked at Ryan who shrugged. "Why would you have to build a house if I came to work here?"

"Because you and Tyler wouldn't want to sleep in the bunk house with all of us who live here and there isn't enough room in this house with Lynzie, Ryan and Jessie in here, so you'd need your own house."

Her heart warmed at his thoughtfulness and she smiled. "Actually, if I were to work here, I wouldn't live here. I already have a home, not too far away."

He seemed to relax a bit at that. "And if, say, a person staying here had an episode where they needed you at night? Would you come?"

She glanced at Ryan who seemed perplexed, but Jessie patted the man's arm. "I think she would. Would you, Meg?"

She nodded. "Of course, but I haven't decided yet."

Ryan stood. "Then it's our job to help you. How about a tour of the farm?"

"I'd like that." She stood and looked down at Tyler. "Are you coming?"

He shook his head. "No, I've seen the place. I'll stay here and chat with your sister and see what secrets about you I can get her to spill. You go. This is your decision." He smiled encouragingly, but there was something holding him back.

"Okay, if you're sure?" She leaned down and gave him a kiss. He lowered her glasses from the top of her head to her nose. "You'll definitely want these."

She squeezed his hand before following Ryan out the door.

It didn't take her long to see what an amazing idea Ryan had. He had already started on a small gym, but most of the therapy was to happen outside with the horses and the upkeep. When he had finished the tour, she was anxious to talk it over with Tyler.

He was standing outside chatting with Jessie and Lynzie, Cooper was nowhere in sight.

"Meg, we came up with a great idea." Jessie smiled, an action Meghan hadn't seen much of before today.

She hooked her arm in Tyler's. "You did? What's the idea?"

He looked at her. "I think we should suggest that Alix come here for her rehabilitation. That way she doesn't have to go home to her dad and brothers and she gets to be on a farm which is what she grew up on. Plus, whether you decided to work here or not, she can still have the benefit of your services."

"Wow, that is a fantastic idea."

"Mind if I suggest it next time I talk to her?" Jessie smirked. "I've kind of been telling her what I'm doing here, and she sounds interested. Maybe if it comes from me, she'd be more likely to say yes."

"I think that's a good idea. Thank you for

thinking of it. Both of you." Her heart filled to see the man she loved and her sister, not just getting along, but working together. It was almost too good to be true.

Ryan pulled his wife against his side. "Have they finished building their case against Drew yet?" He glanced at Tyler. "I know how long those things can take."

Meghan shrugged. "I don't know. They subpoenaed all my notes on him and took my statement and said they'd get back to me if they needed me to testify. I'm not sure, but I think Drew may either plead guilty or be found incompetent to stand trial. I'm not sure which and frankly I don't care." She shivered.

Tyler wrapped his arms around her from behind. "The kid got off easy. If I had caught him before the police—"

Ryan shook his head. "Yeah, I think you would have had to stand in line."

Meghan looked back at Tyler. "Behind Alix's father." His arms tightened around her.

Jessie spit on the ground. "The military is about honor. I hope they throw the book at him."

Lynzie frowned. "I don't understand. Why would a man sign up for the Coast Guard if he has no honor?"

"He had poisoned honor." At Tyler's words, everyone nodded. It made sense in a twisted way.

He unhooked his arms from around her and laid his hand against her lower back. "Are you ready to go home and think about this possible job?"

"I am." She stepped away from him and gave her sister another hug. "Talk to you later."

Jessie nodded.

In no time, she and Tyler were headed back to her place, but his silence was troubling.

She placed her hand on his thigh. "Is something bothering you?"

He glanced at her and sighed. "You are way too observant."

"Only of those I love. Tell me."

He pulled off the road into the dirt parking lot of a closed bar. "I've been thinking about you taking this job and about my job."

"Yes. You know I'm considering it because I feel that counselling people you know may make it difficult for us."

He turned and faced her. "On one hand, I feel guilty about that, but on the other hand, I'm not sorry because I want you in my life."

Oh wow. "You don't have to feel guilty. I feel the same way you do. I'd move mountains to be with you now that I have you."

His whole body relaxed. "I'm glad to hear you say that because there is another subject that has to do with my job that may cause a problem."

"And that is?"

"My next assignment. I'm only here for another sixteen months. I can put in for another year or two here and might get it if I receive that promotion, but after that I don't know where I will have to go."

"So, what are you saying?"

His eyes turned dark and he took her hands in his. "When I get transferred, I want you to come with me. The Coast Guard is very supportive of wives and I think you could easily find another position. We could even discuss together which places we'd like to try for where you could work too."

She stared at him stunned. "Are you asking me to marry you?"

His smile formed slowly. "I guess, I mean, yes, I am. I mean, eventually. You don't have to decide right now. Maybe just live with me and see if any of my habits drive you crazy and then—"

"Oh, my God. Yes!" She threw her arms around him, her heart pounding so hard with happiness it felt as if it should be shaking the truck.

He squeezed her to him then pulled back to look at her. "Wow, I didn't plan that or anything. I don't even have a ring."

Her heart filled with love. "I don't need one. All I need is you." She cupped his face in her hands and kissed him.

His tongue swept into her mouth, promising her

years of love and happiness. She had no doubt, her heart would always be safe with him.

For updates, sneak peeks, and special prizes, sign up to receive the latest news from Lexi at https://app.mailerlite.com/webforms/landing/c1w1g3

Chapter One

I'm pregnant." Lynzie Mullins stared at the word "yes" on the home pregnancy test-strip. Joy, fear, and anger collided inside her.

"Are you sure?" Her best friend, Coco Baker, grabbed the stick out of her hand. "Oh boy, that makes it pretty clear, but I've heard that you should get a real test done by a doctor. These aren't always accurate."

Lynzie took the stick back, still stunned. How could this have happened? Sure, she wanted children someday, but she'd like to have a husband first. Cocktail waitressing wasn't the most lucrative profession, and the only horse farm in town was falling apart, so training horses was out.

"You aren't going to tell him, are you?" Coco's question pulled her back from her worried thoughts.

"Who?"

Coco rolled her eyes. "Andrew. Who else? Unless you've been sleeping with someone other than him. I thought you guys use protection."

"We do." But she'd stopped taking the pill

because of the expense. Besides, Andrew could afford the really good condoms. She flopped down on the couch. Would Andrew help with child support? Would he insist on a DNA test? How much would that cost? Maybe he'd ask her to marry him.

Who was she kidding? He was nice and he liked getting into bed with her, but she knew he considered himself above her. He came from the new section of Lucasville.

They had fun together. It wasn't as if they were in love and while she hadn't slept with anyone while with him, she was pretty sure he had a few other women he saw on a regular basis. A perk of having money.

Coco sat down next to her. "What are you going to do?" Her friend's eyes were honestly concerned. Coco had too soft a heart. She also had a weird ability to recognize people who were soulmates, though she never volunteered that information.

Maybe Lynzie should ask Coco if she and Andrew were soulmates, but she swore she'd never to do that. Everyone bothered Coco about that and as her best friend, she refused to do the same. Besides, she knew the answer already—no. "I don't know. I just found out. I'm still reeling a bit."

"A bit? If it was me, I think I'd faint." Coco laid back over the arm of the couch with the back of her hand on her forehead.

Lynzie smiled. She appreciated her friend trying

to cheer her up. "I think I'll do what you said, go to a doctor. In the meantime, let's keep this between us."

Coco sat up and nodded. "Of course."

They sat in silence a few minutes, Lynzie still staring at the word "yes." It probably wasn't going to magically change to a "no" just because she wanted it to. Sighing, she rose and threw it away.

Coco crossed and re-crossed her legs. She didn't like silence very much. "Not to change the subject, but I'm guessing you won't mind too much if I do. Did you hear that Ryan Crawford came back to town last night?"

Lynzie's heart sped up at the very mention of her old high school crush. "No, I didn't hear."

Coco nodded. "According to Antony, Ryan has come back to help his grandpa sell his old horse farm. I haven't seen him yet, but I hear he looks a lot different."

Just great. "Why? Does he have a limp, burn scars, a big belly? He looked pretty good to me when we were in school."

Coco laughed. "You were the only one who thought so. I think you mixed up his kindness with his looks. That boy was a nerd before they even had a term for it."

She leaned on the counter separating her kitchenette from her living room. "He wasn't that bad. He didn't even wear glasses."

"Well, from what I hear, he's looking mighty fine now. I guess he went into the Army."

"Really? Now how did you find out about that if he just came in last night?"

Coco winked. "I ran into Margot and she said Ryan called Antony about some part-time work at the Love Garage. Want to take a walk and see if we bump into him? You don't have to work until later."

She must be an idiot because she actually considered Coco's idea. "No. I'm sure we'll connect eventually."

"Suit yourself."

If she'd suited herself, she would have run away with Ryan when he first left town. At this point in her life, she wasn't sure if she could handle meeting his wife and kids, if he had them. "Maybe I should—"

A knock at her door stopped her. She stood to answer it, and Coco put her finger to her lips. If it was Andrew, she'd keep the baby stuff to herself…until she'd had a doctor's visit.

She opened the door. "Hello?"

A man with dark hair and a white cowboy hat stood there filling out his blue t-shirt to its max, the outline of his pectorals clear as day. Her entire body took notice.

He smiled, his white teeth gleaming against his tan skin. "Hi, Lynzie."

Huh? A customer from the bar maybe? She would

have never missed such a hot hunk of a man. "I'm sorry, do I know you?"

"I hope so, it's me. Ryan Crawford."

She opened her mouth, but nothing came out. She couldn't stop herself from cataloging everything about him from his very short haircut, to his bulging biceps to the breadth of his chest. "Ryan Crawford?"

He grinned. "Yeah, I've been getting a lot of that today."

She returned her gaze to his mesmerizing eyes. "Oh, my God, Ryan!" She threw her arms around him, beyond thrilled. When his strong arms captured her against his chest, she gave in to the feel of his hard body pressed against her own.

As soon as he loosened his hold, she reluctantly stepped back, old feelings rushing through her. "It's so good to see you. Coco just told me you were in town, but even so, I would have walked right past you in the street and not have known it was you."

"Ahem." Coco cleared her throat.

"Oh, I'm sorry. Come in." She opened the door wider and let him walk by. He took his cowboy hat off and held it in both hands. She closed the door and stepped next to him. "Do you remember Coco Baker?"

He gave her friend a smirk. "How could I forget *hot* Coco."

Coco squinched her nose up at the old nickname

then looked at Lynzie before she cocked her head and studied Ryan from the top of his head to the bottom of his black cowboy boots. "My, my, have you changed."

He grimaced. "So I've heard." Then he grinned. "But you haven't much, though the pink streak in your hair makes me think of peppermint hot chocolate." He winked.

"Oh, come here and give me a hug." Coco wrapped her arms around Ryan, and Lynzie tensed. She shouldn't. Coco was her best friend and for all she knew, Ryan was married, but lost love died hard, at least for her.

When Coco stepped away, Ryan turned toward her. "I'm actually on my way to Antony's place, but I had to stop by and see you. You look good."

She felt her cheeks flush. She looked like crap in her ratty jeans and white tank. She'd thrown her hair up in a clip that morning and hadn't even brushed it. "Thanks. How long are you in town for? I heard you're going to work at the Love Garage."

He shrugged. "Not sure yet about either. Probably through the holidays. I'm helping Gramps get his old Lazy Acres farm ready to sell. It has really gone to h—heck. I figured I'd see if I couldn't bring in a little cash to help pay for repairs. All Gramps has now is his social security."

That was typical for the old locals of Lucasville.

"How great that you're doing that for him." *So, are you married? Do you want to move back here permanently? How do you feel about babies?*

"Lynzie?" Coco caught her off guard.

"What?"

Her friend rolled her eyes then looked at Ryan. "You'll have to excuse her. She didn't get much sleep last night."

That was the truth. "I'm sorry. What did you say?"

Ryan's dark brown eyes seemed to laugh at her. "I wanted to know if you have any time tonight to catch up."

"Oh." Her heart started jumping like a wild rabbit. "I would love—" Coco elbowed her in the side and shook her head. Now why wouldn't she be able to meet—Oh crap, she was scheduled at the pub. "I would love to, but I have to work. Days are better for me. Do you have any time tomorrow?"

Ryan nodded. "Sure. I doubt Antony will hire me on the spot, but they're really busy, so I'm guessing he will eventually. How about lunch tomorrow?"

She smiled. "Perfect."

"Great. I'll pick you up around one. I don't want to take a table for hours from a local business. We have a lot of catching up to do."

Now her heart was jumping harder than a kangaroo. "I'll be ready."

"See you then." Ryan nodded then looked at her

friend. "Coco." He set his hat back on his head and strode for the door.

She stood frozen to the spot until Coco pushed her towards him and she followed. As he stepped out into the sunshine, she held the door open. "Bye."

He gave her a quick smile of his own before descending the stairs to the parking lot below.

She really should close the door, but instead, she watched him until he jumped into a big white pick-up and backed out.

"Get back in here." Coco grabbed her arm and pulled her inside, shutting the door on the hot man that just re-entered her life.

She looked at her friend. "Oh, my God, I can't believe he stopped by. Did you see him? He's gorgeous and built and totally sweet."

Coco laughed. "He sure is. That's one hot cowboy."

Lynzie fell back onto the couch. "His eyes are the same. I always loved his eyes."

"Right, his eyes." Coco chuckled. "So, while you were looking at his eyes, I was looking at his hands."

"His hands?" She frowned. "I didn't notice them. Were they large?"

"Shoot, Lynzie. Come down off cloud nine for a minute. I looked at his hands to see if he had a wedding ring."

She hadn't even thought of that. Suddenly, tingles raced along her skin. "And?"

Coco's smile was smug. "Nope."

She inhaled deeply at the idea that Ryan might still be available then tried to calm down. "He could still be married and not wear a ring or he could have a serious girlfriend or even fiancée." But she really, really hoped he didn't.

Coco threw her hands up. "Could you stop being the pessimist for just a few minutes? Sometimes you drive me crazy with that."

She gave her friend a sheepish smile. "Sorry. Habit. Just too many of my dreams have been crushed. It's hard to have a positive outlook."

Coco dropped down next to her. "I know. I just think there might be hope this time."

She studied Coco, trying to decide if she knew more than she was letting on. Was Ryan her soulmate? She'd sworn she'd never ask. They were too close, and she didn't want to be like half the women in town, pestering Coco to find out if their latest boyfriend was *the one*. Or even going to the mall with her and asking if she could point out their soulmate.

Just as her hope started to rise, she crushed it with her new reality. "But I'm pregnant."

Even Coco's usual cheerful demeanor hesitated in light of that fact. "You don't know for sure. I suggest you make that doctor's appointment and quick."

Ryan parked down the street of the Love Garage, but didn't get out of his truck. He was still recovering from seeing Lynzie again. She'd matured, her gangly teenage body had filled out perfectly. She was still thin and tall, but she had some nice curves he hadn't been oblivious to when she hugged him.

Her face had grown even more beautiful, her green eyes with her naturally long lashes still captivated him. Her full cheeks had thinned, showing off prominent cheek bones, but her nose still had a little point at the end that made him want to kiss it. He was anxious to see how long her hair was. From what he could see, it was darker with less blonde highlights like maybe she wasn't outside as much as she used to be.

She had been the hardest part of leaving Lucasville. She'd also given him the best reception since he returned yesterday evening. Everyone treated him like a traitor or a liar. He wasn't sure which pissed him off more. He was sixteen when his mom divorced his dad and moved them to Florida to live with her parents. It wasn't like he had a choice. The way people in the older part of town were acting, it was as if he'd turned his back on them.

He gripped the steering wheel tighter. It was his father who turned his back on him and Gramps. His grandpa had to be pretty desperate to have contacted his mom and asked for help. The old man was losing it. He muttered to himself a lot and forgot what he was doing. What if he hadn't remembered he had a grandson?

Guilt crept up Ryan's back. For all the resentment he had for his father, he should have at least called his gramps. His mother wouldn't have done anything to keep the relationship going after what his dad had done to her, so he should have made an effort.

Cracking his neck to relieve the sudden tension, he released the wheel. He couldn't change the past, but he was here now and he needed some part-time work if he planned to bring Lazy Acres into saleable condition.

Jumping out of his truck, he walked toward the garage. There were cars parked outside, waiting their turn to be fixed while sounds of rivet guns and country music populated the air through the two open garage bays. The warm weather was an oddity. He would be freezing his ass off in Lucasville soon, especially after living in Florida for so long.

Walking into the chaos that was actually like a well-oiled engine, Ryan felt his blood race. The smell of oil and sight of cars up on lifts reminded him of his days in the Army where working on trucks and tanks had been his oasis…until the day he was wounded.

Still, the sights, sounds and smells of a garage had his hands itching to get dirty.

"Morning, we're pretty slammed today. What's the problem?"

Ryan stifled his grin. Having no one recognize him was getting old, but looking at Antony Love, he couldn't help playing with the man. "Well, I'm pretty sure the transmission is blown. When I shift gears, it's obvious third and fourth isn't working right. Plus, I need new rotors and brake pads, an oil change and my steering wheel is shot."

Antony stared at him, probably counting up the hours and the money it would cost to take care of all those problems. "What kind of car did you say you had?"

"A 1969 GT350 Mustang." He'd always wanted one of those, until he had a chance to drive a tank. Now *that* was real power.

"You're fucking with me. No one in this town has one of those. I'd know."

"Who said I was from here?" Ryan shrugged. "Okay, maybe I'm *from* here, but I just got back."

Antony scowled. "You ass. Ryan Crawford, do you really own a GT350 or are you just making me drool?"

"Just making you drool. But I figured it'd make you happy to know I don't own one either."

Antony shook his head. "Just what I need, a lying mechanic." He studied him another minute but no warm handshake was coming. "Come this way, let's see what you've got. What garage experience do you have?"

"Six years in the Army."

Antony's step hesitated for a second, but he kept walking. "What'd you work on?"

"Mostly Tanks, Strykers and Cougars. A few jeeps here and there, but I fixed pretty much anything they threw at me, including a Black Hawk that wouldn't lift off with a belly full of wounded."

This time Antony did stop and face him. "Overseas?"

He nodded. "Afghanistan."

Antony didn't say anything, but something in his demeanor shifted. Ryan just hoped it was in his favor. There wasn't much else he could do for work if he couldn't work on vehicles. From what'd he'd seen, there weren't any horse farms left in the area that he could hire onto.

They walked over to a small old pick-up truck up on the lift. From the looks of things, the mechanic working on it had just replaced the brake pads. He stepped out from under the vehicle as Antony approached. "I've looked at this thing from front to back and I can't find any freaking leak. Maybe the old geezer spilled coffee in his shed and doesn't remember."

"Coffee?" Antony wasn't buying it.

The mechanic threw up his hands. "You got a better answer?"

Antony looked at Ryan and he got the message. This was a test. He walked by the man and stepped under the vehicle. Methodically, he scanned each part, looking for a possible leak. He loved how everything had its place, one piece fitting between another to work together to make the steel body move. From the undercarriage and the rust, he'd say the truck had to be at least fifteen years old.

He stepped out. "You got a dry rag?"

The mechanic grumbled before walking to a shelf on the wall of the garage and grabbing a rag. Antony stood there, his arms crossed.

When the mechanic came back, Ryan reached for the rag, but Antony grabbed his wrist. "You don't have any grease under your nails." The statement was made like an accusation.

Ryan held his cool by a thread and twisted his arm, breaking Antony's hold. What was wrong with this fucking town that everyone distrusted him? What the hell did he ever do to them, except leave with his mom when she moved away?

He stared Antony in the eyes. "They wouldn't let me work on a vehicle after I got shot until I was good enough to be discharged on my own two feet."

Antony had the grace to look away.

Ryan couldn't care less. He wasn't here to rekindle friendships. He just needed a temporary job and Antony needed some temporary help. That they'd gone to high school together obviously didn't count for squat.

Taking the rag, he wiped it along three separate surfaces, using different areas of it to determine if there was anything coming out that he couldn't see. The three most common places came away dry. He frowned. Overseas, he'd found all manner of strange breaks because the beating the machinery was put through.

A hairline crack could be the beginning of a major failure. It was an old truck and from the dust and grime, he'd say the owner lived in the older section of town, farther out in the boonies. He checked two more spots and still nothing.

If the owner complained of a brown stain… an image of a tank part he'd requisition flashed through his mind, the metal still bearing the stain of human blood from its last life. He hated when he had flashes like that, but in this case, it gave him an idea.

He stepped out and lowered the truck.

Antony just watched him, but the mechanic leaned against a cabinet looking smug. "You couldn't find anything either." The statement pissed Ryan off, so he ignored it. If there was one thing the Army and Afghanistan had taught him, it was to hold his temper.

Popping the hood, he looked around the engine. Then he found what he'd suspected.

When Love Chimes (Broken Valor #1)

ALSO BY LEXI POST

Military Romance

When Love Chimes
(Broken Valor Book 1)
Poisoned Honor
(Broken Valor Book #2)

Contemporary Cowboy Romance

Cowboys Never Fold
(Poker Flat Series: Book 1)
Cowboy's Match
(Poker Flat Series: Book 2)
Cowboy's Best Shot
(Poker Flat Series: Book 3)
Cowboy's Break
(Poker Flat Series: Book 4)

Christmas with Angel
(Last Chance Series: Book 1)
Trace's Trouble
(Last Chance Series: Book 2)

Fletcher's Flame
(Last Chance: Book 3)
Logan's Luck:
(Last Chance Series: Book 4) *Coming 2017*

Paranormal Romance

Masque
Passion's Poison
Passion of Sleepy Hollow
Pleasures of Christmas Past
(A Christmas Carol Series: Book 1)
Desires of Christmas Present
(A Christmas Carol Series: Book 2)
Temptations of Christmas Future
(A Christmas Carol: Book 3) *Coming 2017*

Sci-fi Romance

Cruise into Eden
(The Eden Series: Book 1)
Unexpected Eden
(The Eden Series: Book 2))
Eden Discovered
(The Eden Series: Book 3)
Eden Revealed
(The Eden Series: Book 4) *Coming 2017*

ABOUT LEXI POST

Lexi Post is a New York Times and USA Today best-selling author of romance inspired by the classics. She spent years in higher education taking and teaching courses about the classical literature she loved. From Edgar Allan Poe's short story "The Masque of the Red Death" to Tolstoy's *War and Peace*, she's read, studied, and taught wonderful classics.

But Lexi's first love is romance novels. In an effort to marry her two first loves, she started writing romance inspired by the classics and found she loved it. From hot paranormals to sizzling cowboys to hunks from out of this world, Lexi provides a sensuous experience with a "whole lotta story."

Lexi is living her own happily ever after with her husband and her cat in Florida. She makes her own ice cream every weekend, loves bright colors, and you will never see her without a hat.

www.lexipostbooks.com